C

Operation Dervish

Jack Badelaire

ONE

Five Miles North of the Siwa Oasis, Egypt
November 13th, 1941, 0930 Hours

"Enemy formation ahead! Five hundred yards and closing!"

Corporal Thomas Lynch racked back the bolt of his Vickers machine gun and adjusted his sand goggles, looking over the weapon's sights. Off in the distance, Lynch saw the enemy vehicles; a half-dozen dots staggered across several hundred yards of desert.

"Gunner ready!" he shouted through a kerchief tied across his nose and mouth, trying to be heard over the roar of the Chevrolet truck's engine as the driver shifted into the vehicle's highest gear.

Lynch stood in the back of a 30cwt Long Range Desert Group transport, hanging on for dear life as the truck raced across the Egyptian desert, the driver swerving now and then to avoid rocks or other obstacles. Clutching the twin grips of the Vickers, Lynch tried to keep the weapon steady, a task which seemed to be complete folly, as every bump and jolt along the way caused him to lose his balance and swing the gun around wildly.

"Bend your bloody knees, mate!" Corporal Lawless hollered from the seat in front of Lynch. The New Zealander looked up at Lynch through his own pair of sand goggles and pointed at the Commando's legs. "You gotta move with the truck, not fight against her! Ease up, you're not on a parade field!"

Lynch widened his stance and bent his knees, letting his legs take more of the shock and movement. He immediately felt more stable, the abuse to his spine lessened. He gave Lawless a nod and a thumbs-up.

Lawless lifted his goggles to his forehead and peered through a pair of field glasses. "Three hundred yards! Get ready!"

The LRDG patrolman let the glasses drop, hanging from his neck by a strap, and put his goggles back in place before snapping back the bolt of his Lewis gun, pintle-mounted to the dashboard of the Chevrolet. The driver, another Commando named Higgins, fought to keep the truck steady despite the rough desert terrain.

Lynch pivoted his Vickers gun and brought it to bear on the enemy vehicles as they grew closer. He saw an Italian armoured car in the lead, followed by two German Kübelwagens and three Opel Blitz transports.

"Fire as the target crosses your sights!" Lawless shouted. "Don't try to track 'em as we pass by, you'll just waste ammunition!"

Lynch steadied the Vickers, pointing the weapon ahead and to the left in the eleven o'clock position. Lawless fired first, his Lewis rattling out a short burst. Lynch saw puffs of dust and paint as the .303 calibre slugs ricocheted off the armoured car's hull. Lynch fired as soon as the car entered the sights of his weapon, a ten-round burst that raked the Italian Autoblinda from nose to tail in just over a second. Although he knew the rifle-calibre bullets were no match against the car's armour plating, it would keep the enemy vehicle buttoned up, restricting the crew's visibility.

One by one, they passed a target every few seconds and riddled it with gunfire. By keeping his bursts short and avoiding the temptation to swing the machine gun around and follow the target, Lynch found he was connecting with most of his shots. As the Chevrolet passed the last vehicle, Higgins put them into a wide turn, swinging around the enemy transport, and Lynch watched as Lawless ran his Lewis gun dry, quickly swapping the empty pan magazine for a full one taken from a canvas bag at Lawless's feet. Lynch glanced down into the ammo can attached to the Vickers' pintle mount; the 250-round fabric ammunition belt was roughly one-quarter used. Lynch was pleased with his fire discipline, considering how impossible it would be to try and change ammunition cans and reload the Vickers while staying on his feet as the Chevrolet tore across the desert at combat speed.

As Higgins brought them around for a second pass, this time running up alongside the enemy convoy from behind, Lynch glanced back and saw the other four LRDG vehicles in their formation. The last Chevrolet was passing the Blitz at the rear of the convoy, while the other three trucks were swinging around to continue their gun run. It was important that the last vehicle get out of the first vehicle's arc of fire, lest they find themselves driving through a hailstorm of "friendly" .303 calibre lead.

"Tail car clear!" Lawless shouted at Lynch. "Free to engage!"

Steadying the Vickers, Lynch began his second gun run. The heavy, water-cooled machine gun spat out its deadly payload at a rate of approximately eight rounds a second, and between its great mass and the sturdy pintle mount, the Vickers remained quite steady over level ground, even in his inexperienced hands. Compared to the Thompson submachine gun he normally carried into battle, the Vickers was truly a massive beast, and Lynch couldn't imagine how difficult it must be to carry the huge steel-and-brass weapon, balanced across his shoulders, for hours and days at a time. Or, even worse, having to move from one battlefield position to another, setting the weapon up on its tripod and engaging the enemy while under fire. His Commando squad's Bren light machine gun, normally carried by Trooper Higgins, was a relative lightweight compared to the Vickers.

Within a minute's time they'd passed the Autoblinda armoured car again, Lynch hammering the Italian vehicle with a dozen slugs. Their weapons finally silent, Higgins swung the Chevrolet out in a wide arc to the right, away from the enemy formation, and he brought the truck around so they were facing back towards the remaining LRDG vehicles as they finished their second run, each truck performing the same wheel to the right at the end. Within another minute, all five of the Desert Group trucks were parked abreast, the New Zealanders and the Commandos all congratulating each other on a well-executed manoeuvre.

This was the first live-fire training exercise of the day, but the two units - the Long Range Desert Group and the men of 3 Commando - had been training together ever since their return to the Siwa Oasis headquarters eleven days ago. Before that, the two units had worked together to find and destroy an enemy raiding force hidden in the Libyan Desert. The Axis troops - a company of crack Italian *Bersaglieri* led by a squad of German *Brandenburgers* - had been hunting and ambushing British patrols and convoys for several months. That was bad enough, but the raiders had also posed a threat to the British ability to perform reconnaissance in the deep southern desert regions as their next major offensive drew closer. Lynch had been flown to Egypt along with three dozen other men from 3 Commando, and they'd linked up with the men of the Long Range Desert Group, a reconnaissance unit whose men knew the deep desert better than anyone else. Along with a trio of British armoured cars, the mongrel force had managed to find the Axis raiders and, in a daring night assault, Lynch's squad had infiltrated the enemy's desert fortress and caused chaos as the rest of their comrades struck the death blow, hammering the fortress's defenders with mortars, machine guns, and autocannons. Although the Axis forces had put up a valiant defence, in the end, those who'd survived the assault surrendered to the British, although a handful of the Germans had escaped.

Now, having no further orders, the men of 3 Commando bivouacked and trained with the men of the LRDG. Captain Eldred, the ranking Commando officer, held daily meetings with Captain Clarke of the LRDG and Captain Moody of the 11th Hussars, who commanded the unit of armoured cars attached to the strike force. The men knew something was afoot, but the officers appeared reluctant to share the information, and so there was little to do but train and train some more, all the while trying to acclimatize themselves to the extremes of the desert climate.

The Commandos worked hard to adapt to the searing heat of the day and the frigid chill of night, all the while nursing sunburns and suffering the effects of dehydration. Although water rations at the Siwa Oasis were better than the six pints a day allowed while on patrol, the Desert Group men still maintained a good deal of water discipline, something the Commandos had great difficulty in accepting. The men had been in the damp autumn chill of Scotland only a few weeks before, and a few were laid low by the change, likely to be transported away from the Oasis on the next supply convoy back to the coast. Those who remained found themselves leaner of frame and darker of skin, more than a few joking that, were they to stay in the desert much longer, they'd end up like the mummies entombed under the pyramids.

"Tommy! Oi, Tommy!"

Lynch turned and looked down the line of LRDG trucks to where Corporal Harry Nelson, one of his squadmates, was waving to him.

"What is it now, you great lummox?" Lynch shouted back.

"Pity I didn't have that bloody great autocannon just now. Would've turned those Jerry lorries into scrap-metal!"

Nelson's grin stretched from ear to ear, and Lynch just shook his head. During the assault on the enemy strongpoint,

Nelson had commandeered a twenty-millimetre Breda anti-aircraft gun. The autocannon fired explosive shells from a twelve-round clip, and Nelson had used it to terrifying effect against a squad of *Bersaglieri* charging their position. Most of the squad had been blown apart by the shells, the few survivors huddled prostrate in the steaming offal that'd been their comrades moments before. Nelson had laughed at the carnage the weapon created, and he'd then used the Breda to shred the side of the stone fortress, ripping apart the heavy wooden doors and blasting fist-sized holes in the stone.

After the attack was over, the Commandos and LRDG had stripped the enemy outpost of anything useful, confiscating weapons, ammunition, explosives, food, fuel, spare parts, and even vehicles. The Italians had operated a squadron of six Autoblinda armoured cars, and while three of the vehicles had been too badly damaged to ever drive again, the others were repairable. All six had been brought back to Siwa, the dead cars towed by those still moving under their own power. In addition, those heavy weapons - such as Nelson's Breda autocannon - that still worked were gathered up and brought back to base. The Desert Group patrols weren't especially well-armed, and the firepower acquired in the raid would make a significant difference if they had to engage Axis armoured vehicles in the near future. Given how likely it was they'd be at the forefront of the impending offensive, the "if" of engaging the Axis was more likely a "when".

Turning his thoughts back to the present, Lynch untied the kerchief from his face and shook away the fine dust and sand that'd begun caking the cloth around his nose and mouth. Reaching down, Lynch picked up a canteen, twisted off the cap, and allowed himself three generous swallows, the hot, metallic-tasting water still perfectly refreshing. Letting out a sigh, Lynch twisted back and forth to loosen his back after the beating it'd taken on the ride. Out of the corner of his eye, he noticed a slight hazing to a point on the northern horizon.

Lynch froze. Although he'd only been in North Africa for less than three weeks, he already knew what he was looking at: vehicles kicking up a cloud of dust as they crossed the desert.

"Vehicles approaching from the north!" Lynch shouted.

The banter among the men was silenced immediately, as every neck craned to look, and hands fumbled at the straps of field glasses, trying to get lenses in front of eyes. A murmur of confirmation rippled through the men.

Behind Lynch, Lawless stood with his field glasses glued to his eyes. He let out a grunt. "Armour, at least a dozen, maybe more. Too far away to say for certain."

Two trucks away, Sergeant Highsmith of the Desert Group bellowed at the top of his lungs. "Alright lads, this is no exercise! Nichols, get your truck back to the oasis and tell Captain Clarke we've got company. The rest of you lot, we're going to close and perform recce. Mount up! 'Ere we go!"

"Bloody hell!" Lawless swore. "Tommy, change that ammo belt as fast as you can. We might need a full load!" And with that, Lawless dropped back into his seat and began to reload his Lewis gun.

Lynch snapped open the Vickers' top cover, removed the cloth belt, dropped it back into the ammunition can, then unhooked the can from the mount and fitted a full can in position. Within a few seconds, he had the Vickers charged again with a full two hundred and fifty rounds.

"Gunner loaded!" he shouted.

Higgins dropped the Chevrolet back into gear, and he brought the truck around, pointing north. The four vehicles spread out into a wide skirmish line, Lynch's truck holding the end of the left flank. They accelerated quickly, knowing that against enemy armour, speed was their best - and only - defence. Lynch realized too late his kerchief was hanging around his neck, and he managed to awkwardly fit it over his nose with one hand, the other hanging onto the Vickers for dear life. Higgins was trying his best to avoid the worst of the bumps along the way, but he wasn't as experienced a driver as some of the other Desert Group men, and the distraction of possible violent action in the near future was making the ride exceptionally rough. Lynch bent his knees and tried not to fight against the motion of the truck.

Lawless raised his field glasses again. "They're tanks all right. Sixteen of the great blighters, and they're moving fast!"

"Ours or theirs?" Lynch shouted.

Lawless adjusted the focus and stared for a moment. "Ours, I think. Looks to be Crusaders."

Lynch relaxed a bit. The Crusader was a British "cruiser" tank, lightly armoured and built for speed and maneuverability. While the Matilda tanks he'd seen in action during the Battle of Arras in May of 1940 were "infantry" tanks - slow and heavily armoured to fight the enemy in support of infantry engagements - the cruisers were built for sweeping cavalry-style manoeuvres out in the open battlefield. Although he wasn't schooled in the particulars of armoured warfare, Lynch imagined the North African desert provided the perfect field of battle for the Eighth Army's cruiser tank squadrons.

The Crusaders were moving at a brisk pace, and with the Chevrolet's high speed, within a few minutes the two groups were coming to a stop a few yards apart from each other. Lynch saw the officer in the lead tank's command cupola wore a major's insignia, and the truck crews saluted the officer as he lifted dusty goggles from his face.

"I say, quite dashing of you lads!" the major exclaimed, slapping the steel plate of his Crusader's turret. "Just the sort of fighting spirit I was hoping to find!"

"Sir?" Sergeant Highsmith asked, puzzled.

"Are you in command, Sergeant?" the major asked.

"Of these lads here, yes sir. Captain Clarke is our commanding officer, sir."

The major nodded. "Excellent, then we're right where we should be. Perkins! We're wasting daylight!" the major shouted down into the belly of his tank. The Crusader lurched forward, followed by the squadron's fifteen other tanks.

As the squadron passed through the line of Desert Group trucks and headed south, the major turned and shouted at Highsmith. "Come along now, Sergeant! We've got a war to win!"

Lynch looked down at Lawless and Higgins. The three men were speechless for a moment.

"I don't know who that was or what he bloody well meant," Lawless finally said, "but it can't be good."

"Aye," Lynch replied, "you can be sure of that, now."

Higgins put their truck into gear, and along with Sergeant Highsmith and the other two trucks, followed the mystery major and his squadron of Crusaders.

12

TWO

Bardia, Libya
November 13th, 1100 Hours

Hauptmann Karl Steiner walked through the halls of a former administrative building, passing by Italian and German officers and enlisted men as they went about their business. Steiner exhibited a purposeful stride, his pace unusually quick, his expression determined. Although of only middling rank among the officers moving through the halls, even those senior to Steiner who saw him approach made subtle adjustments to their movements in order to give him a wide berth.

Tall and wiry, with sun-bleached, sandy brown hair and a pleasant, handsome face, Steiner did not look at first glance to be particularly menacing. There was, however, something in Steiner's eyes, a predatory gleam that marked him as a fighting man of no small degree of experience, as did the well-worn look of the leather pistol holster on his belt, and the battered appearance of the desert combat boots on his feet. There was, too, the *Brandenburg* regimental insignia upon his right uniform cuff, and although not every staff officer who

13

saw it recognized the unit, those who did gave Steiner a look of respect, no matter the disparity in rank.

As he continued along his journey, Steiner noticed with no conscious effort the signs of recent battle throughout the building. Bardia had been taken from the Italians by an Australian division back in January, only for the captors to be driven out months later by the Germans. Here and there Steiner saw bullet-scarred stone, plaster, and wood, broken glass that hadn't been replaced yet, and on more than one occasion, the faint but unmistakable stain of old blood on the walls or stone floor, the stains scrubbed repeatedly, but far too tenacious to be defeated by anything save time. Steiner idly wondered how often Bardia would change hands before the war was over.

Finally, Steiner reached the wooden door leading to his destination. A sentry stood guard outside the door, a machine pistol in his hands, but the sentry recognized Steiner and was expecting him. Without a word of greeting, the sentry saluted Steiner and opened the door; Steiner saluted in return as he passed through the doorway.

The office inside was plain and functional. A swastika hung on one wall, a framed photograph of *der Führer* on another. A third wall boasted a large map of Libya and Egypt, with dozens of push pins sporting tiny coloured flags

14

covering its surface, along with small scraps of paper bearing notes of units, dates, and dispositions.

In the middle of the room a plain wooden desk of immense size dominated the space. Steiner measured its proportions with a critical eye and decided the desk had to have been assembled in the room, because there was no way it had fit through either the door or the window. The desk was covered in rolled maps, stacks of reports, a tray with a half-consumed meal, and countless other bits and pieces of administrative debris. Taking it in, Steiner found himself hoping he was never promoted away from the field, because he'd eat a bullet before tackling that much paperwork.

The man whose responsibility it was to tackle the paperwork sat behind the desk. *Herr Oberst* Hirsch was a small, tidy man with thinning light brown hair, piercing blue eyes, and narrow, severe features. Hirsch was one of the staff officers in charge of administering the operations for *Division z.b.V Afrika*, an amalgamation of several infantry units smashed together under one divisional banner and attached to the Afrika Korps. Steiner's Brandenburger company was part of *Sonderverband* - or "Special Formation" - 288, one of the many units that made up this patchwork division. Right now, 288 was in Greece on manoeuvres, sent there while Steiner and his squad were in the deep desert. Now that his command had been wiped out, and he was left with no more than a half-squad of men, Steiner imagined Hirsch had summoned him here to, at best, inform Steiner that he was joining the rest of his company on the other side of the Mediterranean.

At worst, Hirsch was going to verbally rip Steiner apart before having him dragged behind the building and shot for dereliction of duty and incompetence in command.

Hirsch returned Steiner's formal salute and motioned for him to stand at ease. Hirsch held his hands in front of him, resting his elbows on the table, fingers steepled in front of his chin. He looked like an old schoolmaster of Steiner's, who'd ponder at some length before berating the students under his charge. Steiner waited for the first scathing comments.

"*Hauptmann*, I'm going to send you and your men back into the deep desert," Hirsch said.

Steiner blinked. "*Herr Oberst?*"

Hirsch gestured to a letter on his desk. "The Italians are rather distressed at learning we lost a company of their elite infantry and a half-dozen armoured cars. However, we are more concerned with the determination the British showed in finding and eliminating your command in a region of desert nowhere near the active front lines."

Steiner shifted his feet. "Well, sir, we did cause no small amount of trouble to their supply convoys and reconnaissance elements."

Hirsch let out a snort. "So they bring in some of their elite raiding infantry - these *Kommandos* - and risk their precious Desert Group spies to launch a night assault? The last we knew, this raiding unit was in Scotland! You do not fly dozens of men and their equipment such a distance because some supplies are being stolen."

Hirsch's information was news to Steiner, who'd always assumed the Commandos he'd encountered were in North Africa for the same reason he was - unconventional operations. That they'd been brought here just to deal with him and his command stroked his ego no small amount, despite the fact he'd lost against them. Every field commander fantasizes about the enemy sending the very best they had to offer, even though the reality was you always hoped the enemy facing you across the battlefield was made up of cowards and commanded by idiots.

"Sir, if that is the case," Steiner said, "they must have some other goal in mind."

Hirsch nodded. "General Sümmermann has been in discussion with the other division commanders, and the general consensus is, the British are going to launch a major offensive sometime before the end of the year. The questions are where and when. Some feel the British will drive hard for us here at Bardia and seek to shatter the Afrika Korps as quickly as possible, while others think there will be a sweeping manoeuvre through the desert to the south, intending to come up to the West of us and break through to Tobruk, where we've got the Australians trapped."

Steiner nodded. His command had been part of Operation *Sommernachtstraum* back in September, a raiding and reconnaissance mission to find and disrupt the buildup of British forces the Germans knew must be taking place. Unfortunately, there had been little evidence of buildup, and the general consensus at the time was that the British weren't anywhere near ready for such an offensive; if one was to come, it wouldn't be until the end of the year.

Hirsch continued. "Removing your command from its position has blinded us to much of their movements in that area. It is just what we would do, were we to launch an attack from the south and bypass all the defending forces along the northern border between Libya and Egypt. Rommel himself is concerned by any threat that might bring the enemy to Tobruk before we've reduced the defences there and taken the port."

"The generals believe an attack from the south is imminent?" Steiner asked.

Hirsch spread his hands in a prayerful gesture. "Such a possibility cannot be dismissed, *Hauptmann*. And so, this is where you enter the picture."

Steiner stood a little straighter. "What are my orders, *Herr Oberst*?"

Hirsch moved some papers around on his desk. "You're going to be assigned temporary command of a partial armoured car squadron from 33 Reconnaissance Battalion. You'll take this unit south and link up with a unit of panzers from the 15th Division on manoeuvres, where you'll serve under their commanding officer. From there, you'll continue on and make contact with several small depots and installations, appraise their defences and states of readiness, and prepare them for the possibility of a British offensive."

"*Herr Oberst*," Steiner said guardedly, "are we tasked with stopping the British?"

Hirsch chuckled. "No, no, your job is to act as the tripwire, to alert us to any attack from the south. If you encounter hostile British forces, you are to first determine strength and disposition, then break contact and report."

"And then, sir?" Steiner asked.

"And then," Hirsch smiled, "you will transform from tripwire to caltrop. Harass and delay the British as much as possible during their advance until reinforcements arrive. Any questions?"

Steiner snapped to attention and saluted. "*Nein, Herr Oberst.*"

Hirsch returned Steiner's salute. "Then carry on, *Hauptmann*, and good hunting."

Steiner smiled. "*Jawohl, Herr Oberst.*"

THREE

Lynch tried once again to find a comfortable position in the back seat of the Chevrolet truck, then twisted around and looked behind him, squinting into the morning sun rising over Siwa Oasis. The Desert Group base had been his home for a week and a half, but now they were on the move again, departing at first light for the Libyan border. Lynch's Chevrolet was near the head of a formation of several dozen vehicles and well over a hundred men.

The armoured officer encountered the previous morning was Major John Meade, of the 2nd Royal Gloucestershire Hussars. The Hussars were part of the 22nd Armoured Brigade, now part of the 7th Armoured Division, shipped to North Africa in October in preparation for the upcoming British offensive, Operation Crusader. Although Lynch and the rest of the men occupying Siwa had suspected they'd be back in the field again soon, Meade's arrival confirmed everyone's suspicions; Crusader was fast approaching, and they were going to be at the forefront of the action.

21

Last night, the officers had called all the men together and explained Meade's presence. The major was going to take command of the Commandos, the armoured cars under Captain Moody, and the Desert Group patrol under Captain Clarke. These three commands would supplement the major's own Sabre squadron of sixteen Crusader tanks, accompanied by a half-dozen Bedfords carrying petrol, parts, and other consumables. Altogether, these combined elements - nicknamed "Meadeforce" - were to strike out in a north-westerly bearing, cross the Libyan border, and cause as much havoc as possible over the next 72 hours, in the hopes of distracting the Axis forces and diverting some of their manpower away from Operation Crusader's attack corridor.

While at face value it might seem like Lynch and his mates were being left out of the big show, he knew these hit-and-run missions were just the sorts of operations the Commando troops were trained for, and compared to their attack against the *Bersaglieri*, the men of Meadeforce were even more well-equipped. Of the ten Chevrolet trucks, four were carrying heavy weapons: the portee-mounted 37mm anti-tank gun they'd used in the ambush against the Autoblindas and the three-inch mortar they'd used to shell the enemy outpost during the night assault, as well as a captured 20mm Breda and the 28mm "squeeze-bore" anti-tank gun. In addition, each of the trucks not carrying a heavy weapon mounted two machine guns, and carried in its kit one of the massive Boys anti-tank rifles. Although the Boys was big and heavy and kicked like a mule, its .55 calibre armour-piercing bullets were better than nothing against armoured cars or light tanks.

The men were likewise very well-armed. A great number of enemy weapons were captured after the battle at the outpost, and both Commandos and the LRDG men supplemented their personal arms with German or Italian weapons. Lieutenant Price had given one of the other Commandos his Thompson submachine gun, and instead was carrying an Italian-made Beretta Modelo 38 machine pistol. Several other men had acquired Berettas or German-made machine pistols, along with enemy sidearms, grenades, and even several light machine guns. The Commandos - especially those few of Lynch's squad who'd made it out of Calais the previous summer - knew the importance of pilfering enemy arms whenever possible, and from the actions of the Desert Group men, they were no strangers to plundering, either. Resources were simply too tight out in the deep desert to not take advantage of every opportunity to increase one's resources.

In fact, that philosophy went so far as to include enemy armoured vehicles. While they'd captured one Autoblinda before taking the enemy outpost, two more of the Italian armoured cars were salvaged after the battle, and even the remaining dead vehicles were towed back to Siwa. Captain Moody now commanded a makeshift squadron of three Autoblindas and three Morris armoured cars. The British cars were a far cry from the more formidable Italian vehicles, the latter equipped with 20mm autocannons, but beggars such as they were, Moody and his men couldn't complain.

In contrast, Meade and his Sabre squadron were almost immaculate. While no vehicle can cross a significant expanse of North African desert without accumulating a coat of fine sand and dust, otherwise the men and machines looked to be in pristine condition. Their Crusader tanks bore no evidence of battle-damage, and experienced eyes noticed few of the "field modifications" soldiers always made to their vehicles and kit to better suit their role and the environment. It was quickly opined by most of the Commandos and Desert Group men that Meade's Hussars had never, in fact, seen combat.

This notion, more than anything else, tightened Lynch's guts with anxiety. He'd faced long odds several times over the past year, always outnumbered and outgunned. But he'd been led by good men - officers and sergeants baptized in the cauldron of war who emerged to lead men with their wisdom and experience. If Meade and his men hadn't faced off against the Germans before, how could Lynch trust their instincts, their courage? He'd seen men break and run like terrified children during the battle for France, seen officers standing about wide-eyed and gape-mouthed, lacking the slightest notion of what to do. Many of those men never made it to the shores of Dunkirk and back to ol' Blighty. Those few who had, were often quietly and respectfully moved into commands that'd keep them out of trouble, and not put any more lives at risk.

Determined to learn the truth, Lynch waited until the afternoon of the next day, when Meadeforce reached the Libyan border. While the LRDG men cut through the yards-deep barrier of barbed wire, Lynch sought out Lieutenant Price, who was sipping from his canteen, feet propped up against the side of his Chevrolet. Upon seeing Lynch approaching, Price raised his canteen and offered it to Lynch.

"Cold sweet tea, Corporal?" Price asked.

Lynch offered a quick salute that Price casually returned. "No, thank you, sir. Kind of you to offer, Lieutenant."

Price eyed Lynch with amused suspicion. "Why so formal, Tommy?"

"Hoping I might have a word, sir. In private, like." Lynch glanced at the Desert Group navigator in Price's truck.

Price raised an eyebrow but said nothing. Grabbing his Beretta machine pistol from its nook beside his seat, the Commando officer jumped out of the truck and motioned for Lynch to follow him. The pair wandered a few yards away, and after a brief look around, Price slung his weapon and folded his arms across his chest.

"Well, what is it, Tommy?" he asked.

"It's Major Meade, sir," Lynch began. "The lads and I, we're a little uncertain of the major's, ah, bona fides with regards to leading this mission. No offense intended, of course."

Price's eyes narrowed as he looked Lynch in the eye, but the Irishman betrayed no inkling of his true unease. After a moment, Price's expression softened.

"Come now, Tommy!" Price exclaimed with a smile. "As you are quite aware, High Command would never assign an officer to lead a mission without that officer possessing all the experience, faculties, and qualities of character making them the perfect candidate for the job. So you see, Major Meade being assigned to lead this mission is all the reassurance you need as to whether he's qualified or not, because if he wasn't qualified, he'd never have been picked to lead us in the first place!"

Price paused and looked at Lynch with a straight face for all of three seconds, before both men couldn't help it any longer, and they broke into a fit of subdued laughter. Price gave Lynch a friendly pat on the arm.

"My apologies, Corporal, for having a little fun at your expense."

"No worries at all now, Lieutenant," Lynch replied. "That was a right jolly laugh, so it was!"

After a moment the two men regained their composure. Price glanced around again, and seeing there wasn't anyone within earshot, his face grew serious.

"We learned of Major Meade's arrival three days ago. Each of us - Eldred, Clarke, Moody, and myself - tried to reach officers we knew using the RT, to see if anyone could tell us about Meade."

Lynch nodded. He didn't know much about Clarke or Moody's career, but Eldred had been in the Army for many years, and Price's family had connections surprisingly high up the chain of command.

"It seems," Price continued, "Major John Meade has never fired a shot in anger. He graduated from Sandhurst four years before me, and went on to teach armour manoeuvres at Bovington. He's spent the last year petitioning to go into the field, and apparently knows someone with enough weight of metal upon their chest to have finally made it happen."

Lynch's eyes went wide. "You mean...we're going against Jerry and his panzers led by a bloody schoolmaster? This is a mug's game, so it is!"

Price's expression hardened. "I don't like it any more than you do, Corporal. But it's too late to do anything about it, and spreading word of Meade's less than inspiring pedigree will only hurt morale and reduce our chances of making our way out of this alive. Understood?"

"Yes, Sir," Lynch replied, all the while thinking of who he should tell first.

Price could see the wheels turning behind Lynch's eyes. With a sigh, he shook his head.

"As I can already tell you've no intention of keeping this to yourself, at least be prudent. Keep this amongst the Calais men only," Price said.

Lynch nodded. "Aye, Lieutenant."

"I mean it, Corporal," Price added, an edge to his voice.

Lynch gave Price a salute. "Sir, I understand, so I do. Calais men only. We'll not let you down now, so we won't."

Price returned the salute, then turned and walked back to his truck. Lynch began the walk back to his own vehicle, his mind going over how he'd discuss this with the others.

The "Calais men", were the Commandos who'd made it out of Calais in July, when Price's squad was sent back over the Channel to find and bring to England several members of a partisan band who'd caused significant trouble to the occupying Germans since the fall of France. The mission had gone sour when Price, Lynch, and a trooper named Pritchard were captured by an SS officer named Johann Faust, who led an elite unit of *Einsatzkommandos*, SS fanatics trained to hunt partisans and wipe them out. The rest of the squad had escaped capture, but Sergeant McTeague had led the men, guided by the partisans, back into the city on a rescue mission. Pritchard had been executed by Faust, but Lynch and Price had escaped, only to link up with the rest of the squad just as they'd reached Faust's headquarters, deep inside the city.

What followed had been a nightmare journey, the squad fighting a running night battle through the streets of Calais, pursued by Faust's SS as well as the city's regular infantry garrison. Eventually, the Commandos had sought shelter in a half-destroyed church, where they fought a desperate last stand, convinced they were all going to die, before one of the partisans - a young teenage boy - had found a way out of the church's catacombs and into the sewers.

Of the twelve Commandos, only eight survived the Calais mission - Price, Lynch, McTeague, Nelson, Bowen, Johnson, Hall, and White. Ever since, the survivors had begun referring to themselves as the "Calais men", and there was a bond between them that transcended differences in role and rank. The Calais men trusted each other more than the other Commandos in Eldred's command, including those replacements assigned to them, such as Higgins and Herring. Above all else, the Calais men knew that if they stuck together and trusted one another, they could see their way through the hardest fights and the most dangerous missions.

But even the strongest bonds of trust and brotherhood, Lynch knew, were no match for the cold, cruel fortunes of war.

FOUR

Ten Kilometres South of Bardia
November 15th, 1300 Hours

"This mission is utter shit."

Steiner looked up at *Major* Kessler, 15th Panzer Division, as the senior officer spit a wad of brown phlegm over the side of his *Panzerkampfwagen* III.

"I'm sure the *DAK* generals wouldn't be sending us south if they didn't think our mission was important," Steiner said, picking his words carefully.

Kessler gave the younger officer a contemptuous look. "Don't be an ass. We are being sent on a fool's errand. If that peacock Rommel and the others were serious about protecting our southern flank, they would be sending more than this rolling graveyard."

Looking around at their formation, Steiner couldn't help but agree. Aside from a half-dozen Opel Blitzes providing fuel and resupply for the panzers, Kessler's command was made up of vehicles and crews left behind for repairs or recuperation while their units were deployed around Bardia and Tobruk. The armour was a motley collection of seven Panzer IIIs, two Panzer IVs, a lone Panzer II, and even more

31

unusual, a pair of British cruiser tanks, captured and repainted in Afrika Korps colours. One was a relatively new-looking Crusader, the other an older A13, probably captured by the Italians before their allies even arrived in North Africa. All of the vehicles showed signs of combat damage and the hasty repairs made to get them back into the fight. Kessler's comment about a rolling graveyard was probably true - more than a few of these tanks were no doubt the death beds, so to speak, of some of their crews.

The men aboard them now had been a little more fortunate. All the panzer men with Kessler were wounded who'd convalesced in Bardia, and would normally be returning to their units. But now they were thrown together, men crewing panzers who'd never met before a few days ago. Although Steiner was no expert on armour, he knew that, as with a veteran infantry squad, a panzer crew trained tirelessly for months so that they could function together with their vehicle as a single entity, trusting each other and acting instantly as directed by the vehicle's commander. Even if these men were good, dependable soldiers, they wouldn't have formed the bonds necessary to make them truly effective.

If they encountered a veteran British armoured unit, this decision would see good men killed.

Steiner looked back up at Kessler. The major was somewhere in his late 40s - old for his rank, which was troubling - with craggy features and hair turned mostly grey. Kessler's face showed several shiny, bright pink scars that were still healing, and although Steiner didn't ask, he assumed Kessler must've had his last panzer shot out from under him. It was common for veteran crewmen to go through several panzers over the course of a campaign. If they weren't immediately killed by the shot that disabled their panzer, the crew - if they were lucky and well-practiced - could bail out before they burned to death in their vehicle.

"Well, orders are orders," Steiner said in a neutral tone of voice. "I spent months out in that deep desert, and while it wasn't all bad, I can't say I'm particularly eager to go back there."

Kessler looked at Steiner and grunted. "Nonsense. I can see the desire in you. Like a hunting hound, straining at the master's lead, waiting to chase after its prey. You young men are all alike. You think this war will be different. You think our successes in Poland and France mean you are all immortals. But you'll die just the same."

"That is...rather morbid," Steiner replied. "So, you served in the last war?"

Kessler nodded. "From '16 to '18. Gas in my lungs, shrapnel in my back, and a bullet through my thigh. But I lived. I was a crewman in one of the original *Sturmpanzerwagens*, those enormous A7Vs, near the end of the war. It took eighteen men to crew one. Utterly ridiculous. I could probably knock out every one of them with just one of these." Kessler patted the top of his panzer's turret for emphasis.

"I can't imagine what that must have been like," Steiner said. "So many men crammed into a giant steel box. Like a little U-boat rolling across the battlefield."

Kessler laughed. "They weren't anything like a U-boat, trust me. They had no grace to them at all. Got stuck nearly every time you took it off-road, and couldn't cross a muddy trench without burying its nose in the far side. Can you imagine that? How could we have built such a contraption to win that awful war, and it wasn't even able to cross a damn trench? At least the Tommies fared better with their designs in that regard, although not by much."

"Ever fight against British armour in the last war?" Steiner asked.

"Yes, several times," Kessler said. "But oddly, the only shots I ever fired in anger were aboard a captured Mark IV. The Tommies built so many more of those damn things than we did, most of our armoured units fielded *Beutepanzerwagens*, armour looted from battlefields where they'd been bogged down or disabled, then abandoned by their crews."

Steiner pointed over towards the two captured British cruisers. "Some things never change, I suppose?"

Kessler nodded. "They're not as good as our Panzer IIIs, but I'll take them over nothing at all. No sense in letting a fighting machine go to waste."

"Speaking of waste," Steiner glanced at his watch, "I am a little concerned about the hour."

The armoured force was currently parked right outside a supply depot, one positioned in such a way as to support units from Bardia moving to the outer rings of the city's defence, as well as units falling back in need of resupply. Steiner had arrived three hours ago with his temporary command, a trio of armoured cars. He'd been assigned a heavy, eight-wheeled SdKfz 232 and a pair of the lighter, four-wheeled 222s. Steiner had spread his six men evenly among the three cars, rounding out the remaining crew with the vehicles' original drivers. His men were currently sprawled in the shade next to their cars, trying with varying degrees of success to get what rest they could before climbing back into the furnace-hot crew compartments of their vehicles.

When Steiner had arrived, he'd found Kessler's panzer squadron waiting for him. After topping off fuel tanks and water rations before departing, Kessler had informed him they were waiting "for reinforcements". But now, that wait had stretched out into the afternoon, and Steiner worried they'd lose the day sitting here doing nothing.

"Don't be too hasty to rush into a hail of British cannon fire," Kessler replied to Steiner's comment. "Besides, here they come now."

Steiner turned and saw a quartet of Krupp-Protze cargo trucks approaching. He was about to make a snide remark about what he thought of Kessler's reinforcements, when he saw that each truck was towing a Pak 36 anti-tank gun. While they were one of the smaller anti-tank guns in the German arsenal, they were still deadly against the light British cruisers. In the hands of a well-trained crew, the Pak 36 could achieve a good rate of fire, and without all the jostling and lurching of a panzer on the move, the static anti-tank gun could achieve a high degree of accuracy, trading the safety of movement for a very small target profile.

"Alright, *Major*," Steiner said, "these are worth the wait. How did you manage this? I wasn't informed of any anti-tank unit being assigned to travel with us."

Kessler gave him a triumphant smile. "I might be old for my rank, *Hauptmann*, but in all those years, I've acquired a few friends. These are good crews, crack shots, and the Krupp-Protzes are carrying full ammunition loads for their guns."

"What we'll lack in armour, we'll make up in firepower," Steiner replied.

"Indeed. Mount up, *Hauptmann*. We'll be departing shortly."

Steiner saluted Kessler and walked to his armoured car. Opening the side hatch, he squeezed himself inside the body of the SdKfz 232 armoured car. Nodding to his men, Steiner made his way into the turret and poked his head and shoulders above the rim of the commander's hatch. Over his head, the large "bedframe" radio antenna was draped with a light-coloured canvas sun shade, a field modification Steiner knew he'd appreciate over the next few days.

Gefreiter Werner, one of Steiner's remaining Brandenburgers, looked up at him from inside the belly of the car.

"The other men...they are concerned," Werner said in a low voice.

Steiner made a dismissive gesture with his hand. "I think *Major* Kessler is more cunning than he might seem at first glance. I had my concerns as well, but I do not think he is incompetent. I believe he is an old war hound who prefers the thrill of the hunt to the warmth and safety of the hearthfire."

"*Das ist gut*, but this mission..." Werner continued.

"You did not join this regiment expecting an easy war, did you?" Steiner asked. "We will do as we are told, but rest assured, I intend to grow old and die in bed, with a *Fraulein's* plump bosom for my pillow."

"Right now, I'd settle for a bottle of *Korn* and a good night's sleep," Werner replied.

Steiner chuckled. "Now, now, such fantasies! Let's be realistic!"

A moment later, Kessler gave the order to move out, and Steiner ordered his three armoured cars to spread out far beyond the front of the formation, to serve as the eyes and ears of Kessler's force.

Damn him, Steiner thought, *it does feel good to be hunting again.*

FIVE

Thirty Miles West of the Egypt-Libya Border
November 16th, 0530 Hours

Corporal Rhys Bowen shifted his Lee-Enfield sniper rifle three degrees to the left, and the Axis supply depot slid into view. The thread-thin webs of barbed wire were just barely visible in the predawn light, but there was no missing the large brown tents, the stockpiled fuel cans and ammunition crates, the *sangars* draped in camouflage netting as much to shield their occupants from the sun as to make the gun emplacements harder to target from the air. Several boxy Fiat cargo lorries were parked inside the depot's perimeter, as well as a pair of Autoblinda armoured cars and a lone M13/40 tank. The three armoured fighting vehicles were parked nose-first into their own *sangars*, the piled rocks and sand providing them with passable hull-down positions. Given the size of the depot and the number of tents and fighting positions, Bowen estimated the enemy's strength at somewhere near a reinforced platoon.

Around the depot, there were signs of early morning activity. A thin wisp of smoke rose from a cooking fire, and Bowen made out men walking around, pulling on coats to fight off the early-morning desert chill. Although their movements seemed casual and unhurried, Bowen saw the Italians were carrying their rifles and machine pistols wherever they went, and more than once, he spotted a man Bowen took to be an officer or NCO stop near the wire and scan the eastern horizon with a pair of field glasses. *So, they are wary, but don't feel an attack is imminent,* Bowen thought to himself.

Contrary to the opinion of the average soldier, the role of a sniper in war was less about killing the enemy, and more about infiltration and intelligence gathering. Trained in stealth, stalking techniques, and how to observe and acquire information about the enemy, those skills were often more useful to a sniper's commanding officer than the ability to shoot a man dead at extreme distances. To Bowen, the measure of a good officer was how intelligently they made use of Bowen's talents, recognizing and employing the full range of his abilities, and not just the mating of trigger and finger.

The previous evening, five miles from where Bowen now lay, Major Meade had pointed out the location of their first target - an Italian supply depot. Intended to support German and Italian reconnaissance units, it had been spotted by the RAF and marked for destruction with a bombing run. However, once their operation entered the planning stages, the supply depot was picked for another purpose. A recce flight had photographed the depot, and in the photos, a long-range radio transceiver antenna was visible. Knowing the Italians were able to make radio contact with someone further up the Axis chain of command, their choice as the first of Meade's targets became assured.

Three hours ago, with little more than a compass bearing and their training in night manoeuvres, Bowen, his spotter Johnson, and four other Commandos had set out into the desert, tasked with finding the supply depot and reporting back on its defences. They'd begun their trek an estimated three miles from the depot, and by Bowen's current reckoning, that distance was accurate to within a quarter-mile.

"Sunrise?" Bowen whispered, not taking his eye from the rifle's scope.

He felt Johnson shift slightly next to him. Both men were prone, with a ragged-looking desert bush between them and the depot. While it would provide no cover against enemy fire, it helped break up their outline if anyone was scanning the area with field glasses.

"Fifteen," Johnson whispered.

Even this far away from the enemy, the two men made as little noise as possible. Both trained together constantly, and by now they were at a point where their communication was largely reduced to slight gestures or single words, all intended to reduce their chances of being spotted.

"It's time," Bowen said. Johnson shifted, rolling onto his side and pulling an electric torch from his satchel. Johnson pointed the torch directly behind them.

"Estimate five-zero Italians," Bowen said, "no Germans visible. Two MGs, possible mortar, wire, two armoured cars, one light tank. No A-T visible. RT confirmed."

Johnson slowly repeated the words as he flashed the torch in the direction of the pale dawn horizon. Half a mile to the east, one of the four men they'd departed with lay alone in the sand, watching for Johnson's coded signal and repeating it with another torch. The process was repeated until the message reached the main body of the Meadeforce, at which point the message was acknowledged with the single flash of a torch back to the west, repeated up the chain until Johnson spotted it with his field glasses.

"Received," he said to Bowen. "How long d'you think?"

"With Major Meade in command, they'll be along momentarily," Bowen replied. "He's straining at the lead like a terrier on the scent of a rat."

A moment later, there was a low rumble from the east, a sound not unlike the roll of distant thunder. The rumbling grew louder, and even miles away, the faint squeal of high-speed machinery was audible. Peering through the scope,

Bowen saw the first gleam of morning sunshine reflecting off of the depot's radio transmission tower. As the seconds passed, the sun's rays slid lower, like a burning fuse, and within a minute the sunlight touched the turret of the Italian tank.

At almost the same instant, the Italian garrison began to notice the sound of approaching motor vehicles. Men turned to the east, squinting into the morning sun as it began to climb up over the horizon. Bowen felt Johnson shift as the spotter looked behind them.

"Bloody perfect," Johnson said. "You can't see a thing with the sun in your eyes."

Bowen continued to watch through the scope as the Italians began to mobilize. Cups of coffee were poured down throats, men tossed aside what remained of their breakfasts and ran towards their defensive positions. A tank crewman climbed up onto the track guard of the M13/40, heading for the turret.

"Time to earn the King's shilling," he said to Johnson.

Although his target was at the extreme end of the Lee-Enfield's practical, effective range, Bowen was one of the best marksmen in 3 Commando, his rifle hand-picked from dozens of other specimens for the serendipitous mating of barrel, stock, trigger, and other components that gave it superior accuracy. Bowen's finger slowly squeezed the trigger until it broke, the *crack* of the rifle's report and the recoil against his shoulder something of a surprise, as it always was with a proper killing trigger pull. Though only a few inches above the sandy ground, the rifle's muzzle blast raised little dust - a canvas drop-cloth had been laid out in front of Bowen's shooting position, preventing the high-pressure gasses from kicking up a cloud of sand, which would not only obscure his view, but give away his position.

Bowen's aim was impeccable. Just as the tank crewman reached the top of his turret, the .303 calibre bullet arrived and caught him low in the back. The tanker threw his hands out and staggered for a moment, before toppling face-first over the turret and sliding out of sight.

"Scratch one Eyetie," Johnson murmured, as he watched through his field glasses. "New target, left twenty yards, leftmost armoured car, right side."

Bowen shifted and immediately saw a man beginning to climb into the side hatch of an Autoblinda.

"On target," Bowen replied.

Resisting the urge to rush the shot, Bowen spent an extra half-second to steady his aim, and was rewarded when the Italian's left leg buckled, the bullet smashing into the man's thigh with more force than a sledgehammer's blow. The Italian crumpled to the ground next to the armoured car, clutching his shattered leg.

"Right, he's out of it. New target, shift left ten yards, MG emplacement," Johnson said.

The *sangar* emerged from the left side of the scope's field of view, but the shade of the camouflage netting made identification difficult.

"No target," he said to Johnson.

"I saw the blighter duck in there, give it your best."

Bowen took an educated guess and fired a round over the dark shape of the machine gun. A moment later, the MG's barrel jerked to the side, much as if a body had suddenly slumped against the weapon.

"That's a hit," Johnson confirmed.

By now, the Italians were fully aware of the unseen marksman picking them off one by one. The second machine gun began to fire, sweeping wide arcs of tracer-lit fire through the air. But the Italians couldn't see where the shots were coming from, had no idea of direction or range, and the few rounds that strayed anywhere near the two Commandos sailed well overhead.

"New target, second MG emplacement, shift forty yards right."

For the next few minutes, as the sounds of the approaching Meadeforce grew louder behind them, Bowen and Johnson worked together as sniper and spotter, engaging target after target as fast as Johnson could find them and

Bowen could work the bolt of his Lee-Enfield. The volume of fire coming their way was increasing dramatically, perhaps because the Italians had figured out they were using the rising sun to conceal themselves, but the enemy's shooting was random and unfocused, sprayed out into the dawn in the vain hope of spoiling his aim. Bowen, however, wasn't overly concerned with machine gun fire, especially panic fire like he was seeing now, most of the shots impacting dozens or hundreds of yards short, or so far above them he'd still be safe standing straight up.

It was as his father, a sniper in the last war, had said to Bowen while teaching the young boy how to shoot. *A hair's width or a mile, makes no difference at all if you miss 'em.* The first time Bowen had come under fire, during the battle for France last year, his father's words had been in his thoughts, and Bowen had taken comfort in them. Instead of freezing up at the sound of bullets snapping past his head, the young man had treated it as a problem to solve, one of geometry and angles, distance and drop, the science of ballistics comforting him in its precision. As long as you made sure you were not somewhere along a bullet's trajectory, the bullet could not harm you. Stay out of firing arcs, use cover, present as small a target as possible, and the odds would tip in your favor to the point where you were in control of your fate, not the man at the other end of the gun.

On the other hand, mortars, artillery, and bombs - now, those scared Bowen. There was no science to their slaughter, no way to precisely measure how they killed. While you could determine where a bomb or shell would land to some degree of accuracy, the explosion and fragmentation killed seemingly at random. Bowen had seen men killed by a tiny fragment of shrapnel from a blast fifty feet away, while a mortar bomb landing ten feet away did no more than muss another man's uniform. Luck was the only thing that saved a man from the crushing blast waves and the razored edges of shell fragments, and Bowen did not trust luck. It was a fickle thing, a will-o'-the-wisp, the forlorn hope of brave fools who charged into enemy fire with fixed bayonets. That was everything a sniper was not, and so Bowen trusted only in his training, his spotter, his rifle, and the best pair of eyes God ever gave to a Welshman.

Bowen felt Johnson shift next to him as the spotter glanced behind them.

"Here come the rest of the lads, and not a moment too soon. Air's getting a bit thick."

The suppressive fire from the Italians was indeed getting heavier, and although neither man had been hit, a few branches from the bush they were hiding behind had been knocked away by near misses. Now, Bowen heard the growl of Chevrolet truck engines and the squealing clatter of armour louder than ever, racing across the desert and approaching from behind them.

Pausing to feed another stripper clip of five rounds into his rifle, Bowen rolled onto his side and glanced back over his shoulder. Spread out over a distance of at least a quarter-mile, the ten LRDG trucks and the half-dozen armoured cars were coming towards them at top speed. A half mile behind this first wave, the sixteen Crusaders of Meade's sabre squadron were cutting across the desert in a broad V formation. An alarming thought suddenly came to mind.

"Let's hope they're awake at the wheel," he said to Johnson. "I don't fancy tyre treads up my backside!"

"Should I flash my torch at them?" Johnson asked.

Bowen shook his head. "They're too trigger-happy. Probably take it for muzzle flash and riddle us full of bullets. I'll keep an eye on the Italians, you give our lads a wave if they get too close."

Rolling back into position and getting back on the rifle, Bowen saw through his scope that the Italians, despite the casualties and confusion he'd caused, were preparing to meet the vehicles they now saw bearing down on them. The turrets of the armoured cars and the lone tank began to move, and Bowen saw a flash of smoke and flame from the tank's muzzle a moment before he heard the boom of the gun. The sound of tearing cloth cut through the air over their heads, and

Bowen heard several replies from the Crusaders' two-pound guns. One of the shells missed entirely, impacting hundreds of yards past the depot, while another smashed to kindling a stack of crates near the Italian tank. The third shell impacted on the *sangar* in front of the tank, sending fragments of stone flying for yards in all directions. Through his scope, Bowen saw an Italian running past the tank cut down by a stone fragment, the missile striking the unfortunate man in the head and dropping him as if he was shot through the skull by Bowen's rifle.

The Italian tank fired its cannon again, and this time, Bowen heard the shot smash home behind him a moment later with a great metallic clangour.

"Bloody hell!" Johnson exclaimed. "That bunch of poor buggers are done for!"

Bowen risked taking his eyes off the glass for a moment and glanced over his shoulder. To his horror, he saw an LRDG truck in the process of catastrophically coming apart - men, weapons, supplies, and vehicle parts tumbling across the desert at forty miles an hour.

"The shot took them right in the bonnet. Blew out the back end like nothing was even in the way," Johnson muttered, eyes wide and unblinking.

Bowen shook his head and hoped none of the men from his squad were on board that truck. Pity for the others, of course, but it was always easier when you barely knew their names.

The trucks began to race by their position, tracers spitting from their machine guns as they came within effective range of the Italians, who answered the challenge with machine gun and autocannon fire. Bowen saw a pair of 20mm cannon shells blow holes in the side of a Chevrolet truck big enough for him to stick his head in, but he didn't see any of the truck's occupants slump or tumble off, so he figured they weren't wounded, at least not badly. The same couldn't be said for a Commando manning a Vickers gun in the back of another truck; the man was caught in the path of an Italian machine gun's tracers and flung off the back of his vehicle, tumbling across the sand like a rag doll. Bowen couldn't tell at that distance who the man was, and hoped it wasn't his friend Tommy Lynch, who held a similar position on one of the trucks.

"So long, tossers!" shouted a man from the back of the truck passing closest to their position. Bowen saw it was Harry Nelson, hanging onto the 20mm Breda autocannon portee-mounted to the truck bed. Nelson waved and shot them a rude two-fingered gesture as the truck sped past, the cloud of dust kicked up by its passage causing Bowen and Johnson to choke and cough.

"Nelson, you bloody maniac!" Johnson hollered back.

Bowen sighed and began to stand up. "C'mon, on your feet. No one's shooting at us anymore, and I don't fancy getting squashed by those tanks when they get here in a moment."

Johnson got to his knees and began packing their kit. Ahead of them, machine guns and cannons hammered out lead as engines roared. The ginger-haired spotter grimaced and spat out a dust-coloured wad of phlegm.

"Harry's the bloody tosser," Johnson muttered.

Bowen shrugged and checked his rifle, making sure a live round was chambered. The two men began to walk towards the Italian depot as the first Crusader tanks thundered past them.

"He can shag sheep for all I care," Bowen replied. "As long as he keeps that damn cannon of his pointed in the right direction."

SIX

Harry Nelson was a man of simple pleasures. Chasing skirts, draining pints and drams, putting the boots to Jerry whenever he could - these were the things that brought a smile to his face. But more than a fine pair of big round Bristols, or a foaming pint of stout, or some poor German with a bullet in his belly, Nelson found pure, almost divine joy in blowing Eyeties all to bits and gobs with the great big bloody autocannon of theirs he'd pinched from the *Bersaglieri* fortress two weeks ago.

Nelson spun the traversing wheel of the 20mm Breda 35 autocannon, swinging the weapon's barrel around and pointing it at the two o'clock position as he prepared to blast the Italian depot. He slapped the clip of twelve high-explosive cannon shells one more time, making sure they were properly seated, and he yanked on the cannon's charging handle, chambering a shell. The muzzle of the Breda bounced and jerked as the Chevrolet truck it was mounted onto raced across the desert at over thirty miles an hour.

52

"Keep 'er steady, you berk!" Nelson shouted at Trooper Herring, who immediately took one hand from the wheel to offer up a two-fingered retort without bothering to look behind him.

"Bloody wanker!" Nelson groused under his breath. Within seconds, the truck was passing along the left-hand edge of the supply depot, and the closest machine gun emplacement entered Nelson's sights.

With a maniacal grin on his face, Nelson opened fire. The muzzle blast was terrific, the ball of fire leaping from the weapon almost a yard in diameter. Like an enormous steam-hammer, the cannon thumped back against its mounting over and over, its motion rocking the truck on its suspension. The first couple of shells were too early, either glancing off the angled stone front of the *sangar* or missing altogether, but with a few deft corrections using the aiming wheels, Nelson got the gun on target, and kept the weapon traversing as the truck passed by the emplacement.

The results were spectacular. The rest of the cannon's twelve-round clip sent pulverized stone flying through the air, along with shredded chunks of meat and bone, only identifiable as the remains of human beings because of the bits of uniform cloth and personal kit mingled with the once-living debris. Within seconds, the well-constructed defensive position, as well as the machine gun and its crew within, were utterly destroyed.

Nelson looked upon the damage he'd done with satisfaction. He felt no particular enmity towards the Italians; they weren't as bad as the Germans, especially the fiendish SS they'd dealt with in Calais. But on the other hand, Nelson didn't have any sympathy for the men he'd just killed, either. They and the rest of their countrymen had bought into Mussolini's schemes, his desire to revive a new Italian empire as grand as their ancestors'. When Nelson had heard Mussolini boasted of his army's "eight million bayonets", Nelson had laughed out loud, picturing the poor Eyetie infantry marching into the teeth of emplaced machine gun fire, mortar bombs exploding, tank treads grinding men into ragged meat.

Bayonets or no, Nelson had to admit the Italians could be brave soldiers. As he sped past the left flank of the supply depot, men knelt and fired at him, rifles and machine pistols filling the air with lead. He heard the snap-crack of bullets going past his head, and the body of the Chevrolet rang with the impact of high-velocity metal. Nelson unfastened the clip of expended cannon shells from the side of the Breda and fitted a fresh load, just as a piece of the truck body the size of a dinner platter disintegrated a few feet away. One of the Autoblinda armoured cars was tracking them with its own

Breda autocannon, and Nelson felt the buffet of air as a cannon shell passed by him.

"Kill that bastard, Harry!" their Kiwi navigator screamed at him from the front of the truck. Nelson frantically spun the traversing wheel, swinging the muzzle of his cannon about, trying to keep it lined up with the Autoblinda. The armoured car's turret was rotating as well, each gunner in a race to see who could lay sights on the other first.

Fortunately, Nelson was the winner. As soon as the Breda's sights touched the rear of the armoured car, Nelson opened fire, relieved to see the high-explosive cannon shells flying true, slamming into the thin rear armour plating of the Autoblinda. The HE shells detonated across the car's engine compartment, sending bits of steel spinning through the air, leaving fist-sized holes behind. The armoured car's hatches slammed open and several crew members stumbled out, gouts of thick black smoke following behind them.

By now, Nelson's car was completely past the supply depot, and Herring executed a wide turn to the left, taking them out of harm's way as the squadron of Crusader tanks bore down on the enemy position, their machine guns blazing away. Nelson watched the approach of British armour with fascination, wondering what it must be like to have control over one of the steel behemoths. Although spread out on a wide front, at least five or six hundred yards across, the tanks were able to lay fire on the Italian's position; machine gun bullets chewed through piles of crates and riddled barrels filled with petrol. Fires brewed up everywhere as tracer rounds ignited flammable materials, and the Italian infantry found there was nowhere to hide where British machine gun fire couldn't find them.

And where mere bullets couldn't penetrate, the armour-piercing shot of the Crusaders' two-pounders smashed through with impunity. The lone Italian tank managed two more shots from its 47mm cannon, one of them scoring a direct hit against a Crusader's track guard. Hunks of steel plate and wrecked track links spun through the air in a puff of dust and sand as the armour-piercing shell smashed home, and the racing tank slewed around, coming to a halt with its shattered track dragging behind. In retaliation, the wounded Crusader fired two shots in rapid succession, and its fire was joined by two other nearby tanks.

The storm of high-velocity steel rounds tore the M13/40 to pieces. Nelson watched in fascination as the two-pounder AT shells punched through the Italian tank's armour, smashing holes in the front glacis plate and turret. As the tank began to burn, the top hatch popped open and a lone Italian tanker bailed out, only to be shredded by MG fire from the crippled tank. Nelson felt an uncustomary moment of pity as he watched the man try and escape the smouldering iron coffin of his tank, only to be cut down a moment later. He reminded himself that if the roles were reversed, the Italian would likely do the same thing to the British tankers opposing him. A second later, the Italian tank shuddered repeatedly as its cannon shells began to cook off and explode, thick clouds of oily black smoke and white-hot flame erupting out of the open turret hatch.

With the death of their only tank, the Italians decided they'd had enough. Men began to throw down their rifles, and a white rag on the end of a rifle barrel poked out of the hatch of the surviving armoured car, waving furiously. Over the next minute, the Crusaders, the armoured cars of the 11th Hussars, and the LRDG trucks slowly closed in around the depot, occasional bursts of submachine gun or MG fire delivered into the ground, herding the Italians as a sheep dog might guide its flock.

Nelson reloaded his Breda cannon, then climbed down from the bed of the truck, Thompson in hand and ready. The other Commandos were dismounting from their vehicles, weapons trained on the dozen or so Italians still on their feet and huddling in the middle of their camp, arms raised, heads tucked meekly into their shoulders. Only one of the Italians seemed the slightest bit indignant, and to Nelson, the man had the bearing and uniform decorations indicating some kind of officer's rank. Captain Eldred moved towards the

Italian officer, limping slightly from an old wound, a trooper whose name Nelson didn't know accompanying him. Nelson recalled the trooper spoke Italian to the *Bersaglieri* they'd captured two weeks ago, and Eldred began talking to the enemy officer, using his man as an interpreter.

Suddenly there was a great shout of consternation from one of the Crusader tanks, and Nelson turned to see Major Meade jumping down from the tank's turret, face crimson.

"Hold it right there, Captain!" Meade shouted at Eldred. "This is my command, and if anyone is going to accept this man's surrender, it's bloody well going to be me!"

Eldred halted in mid-sentence, and turned to Meade, face unreadable. "My utmost apologies, Major," Eldred replied. "I thought you might be preoccupied by other duties."

Meade strode up to Eldred, looking down his nose at the shorter Commando officer. "Other duties, you say? What the hell duties are more important for the commander of this expedition than accepting the formal surrender of a defeated enemy?"

Eldred blinked twice. "Pardon, Major. I presumed you'd want to take reports from all the elements under your command, coordinate the tending to of our dead and wounded, make sure our perimeter is secure..."

"I'll leave that for junior officers such as yourself, *Captain*." Meade waved his hand as if to shoo away a bothersome insect. "In the meantime, leave your man with me so I can carry on a civilized conversation with this gentleman."

Nelson, watching from a dozen paces away, admired Eldred's composure. If it'd been him suffering under Meade's imperious glare, Nelson would have been hard-pressed to hold back from knocking the major's teeth down his throat. Still, Eldred's expression and body language was positively murderous as the Commando officer saluted Meade, pivoted smartly, and strode away. As he walked past Nelson, Eldred gave him a glance, and although it only lasted a moment, Nelson knew if he'd been Major bloody Meade, he'd have caught fire from the heat of Eldred's wrath.

As Eldred walked away, heading towards where Lieutenant Price and Captain Moody were talking near the armoured cars, Nelson turned and caught the eye of Sergeant McTeague, standing next to his Chevrolet car nearby.

"Oi, Sergeant," Nelson said softly, "we got ourselves a whole kettle o' trouble brewing up."

"Aye laddie," McTeague replied, eyeing Meade as the major waved his arms in the air, cursing in frustration at his translator, "and it's going to be a bitter brew, that's for sure."

"Just hope we don't bleedin' choke to death on it," Nelson muttered, and strode off, hoping to find a choice bit of loot before any of the other lads got to it.

SEVEN

One Hundred Fifty Kilometres South-West of Bardia
November 16th, 0615 Hours

Major Kessler re-read the message scrawled across the paper in his hand and looked down from his panzer's turret at Steiner.

"Your man, he speaks Italian well? He didn't misinterpret the message?" Kessler asked.

Steiner shook his head. "Werner is fluent in Italian, and I speak it almost as well. When I heard the Italian radio operator resend the message, even though it was very faint, I made out the details clearly enough to know Werner wrote them down correctly."

"*Scheisse*," Kessler muttered. The grizzled officer let out a lengthy sigh and scratched the stubble on his chin. "Hand me your map."

Steiner unbuckled his leather map case and pulled out the relevant map, handing it up to Kessler, who unfolded it while gesturing for Steiner to climb up next to him. The two men looked over the features and coordinates on the map for a couple of minutes before Steiner jabbed a finger against a point on the map south of their current position.

"There. I know the place," Steiner said. "While we were operating in the deep desert, this was one of the depots near our position, and when we'd receive new shipments of consumables, they'd come from there."

"How large was the garrison?" Kessler asked.

"A full platoon of Italians, plus a few extra men from their supply company. There were always a few armoured cars or tanks passing through and resupplying. Maybe forty to fifty men, depending on the day."

Kessler's finger tapped the message paper next to the map. "A platoon and maybe a few armoured cars, against 'a large enemy attack force of armed trucks, armoured cars, and fast-moving tanks'. I don't give the Italians much of a chance."

Steiner shook his head. "Nor do I. These were garrison troops, not *Folgore, Alpini,* or *Bersaglieri.* They'd put up a brave fight to appease the officers, and then fold at the first sign of being hopelessly outgunned. If they weren't exaggerating in their message, and there was more than a troop of armoured cars or tanks, they'd have no chance."

"Are we the nearest friendly unit?" Kessler looked over the map, his finger wandering across the paper, as if in search of reinforcements.

"There is an aerial reconnaissance station, an airfield located seventy kilometres south of us," Steiner said, pointing to its location on the map. The point was almost exactly halfway between their position and the Italian depot.

"Do you think they'd have heard the distress call?" Kessler asked.

"The station is manned by Germans," Steiner replied. "If we heard it this far away, there's no chance they missed it."

Kessler nodded. "They'll have a Storch in the air by now, heading towards the depot. Try and raise the airfield, inform them of our approach. We're going to push hard and get there as fast as we can."

Ten minutes later, the panzers and their support vehicles were on the move again. Steiner's radio operator had raised the airfield, and as Kessler had predicted, a Storch was already airborne, heading in the direction of the depot. The airfield's radio operator assured them a report would be radioed back as soon as the reconnaissance flight returned.

An hour later, Steiner received word of the Storch's report. A great deal of smoke was seen coming from the depot, and the reconnaissance flight identified at least two plumes from wrecked vehicles, as well as a number of fires from destroyed fuel stocks and other supplies. Of the British, the Storch crew spotted at least a squadron of tanks - sixteen or more - as well as a number of armoured cars, both British and Italian, although the nature of the war in North Africa meant the nationality of a vehicle had little to do with who built it and fielded it in the first place. At the time of observation, all the British vehicles were surrounding the Italian depot, and there were no signs of an ongoing battle. Steiner knew that, given the numbers involved, the fight would have lasted only a few minutes.

The Storch's crew also mentioned seeing a number of armed light trucks, of the kind most often associated with the British desert scouts, the Long Range Desert Group. This gave Steiner pause; men driving such vehicles were at least part of the assault force that had engaged his armoured car patrol, knocking out three of his Autoblindas. The British Commandos he'd met under a flag of truce also drove a similar vehicle, and while it had been too dark to know for sure the night the Commandos attacked his outpost, he knew some of the attackers were using armoured cars and light trucks.

Could the men who'd just taken the Italian depot be part of the same unit his men and the *Bersaglieri* had faced two weeks ago? It seemed at least plausible. Steiner knew the British Desert Group focused on gathering intelligence, not carrying out raids, and this was the same region of the desert. If they were fighting in support of British "cruiser" tanks, armour fast enough to keep up with the recce vehicles, this could be a British reconnaissance in force along the southern corridor, maybe even the lead elements of a larger, slower, combined-arms force. It could be the exact situation the *DAK* commanders sent them here to discover. What had seemed like a waste of men and armour now appeared to be a much more dangerous venture.

Several hours later, after pushing their vehicles as fast as they dared, the armour column reached the airfield. A dozen camouflaged tents of various shapes and sizes surrounded a tall radio tower, all of it guarded by a handful of *sangars* also covered in camouflaged netting. A short airstrip of clear, flat desert had been bulldozed next to the tents, a tan-coloured Storch reconnaissance plane sitting at one end with a refueling truck doing its job alongside. As Steiner's car slowed to a stop near the outermost tents, several men in various uniforms approached warily, all of them armed. At their head was a young man in the uniform of a *Luftwaffe Oberleutnant* carrying an MP-40 at the ready.

Steiner stood up fully in the cupola of his 232 so the officer could see his uniform. "Are you in command here?" he asked the young officer.

The *Oberleutnant* gave a salute, which Steiner returned. "*Oberleutnant* Hasek. I am in command of this airfield."

"Not any more, *Oberleutnant*. I am *Hauptmann* Steiner, and *Major* Kessler will be here momentarily." Steiner gestured behind him, towards the rapidly approaching panzers. "We have reason to believe your installation may be the next target for the British force to the south."

"I wasn't told about this by my superior officers," Hasek said, a dubious look on his face. "And this is a *Luftwaffe* command. You have no authority over us."

Steiner shook his head. "This war moves too fast to sit around waiting for orders from someone on the coast. We were sent south to catch any British forces hoping to sneak in behind our lines from the deep desert, and it appears we've found them. Your airfield is the only target within striking distance of that supply depot. We're going to make this our base of operations, find the British through aerial reconnaissance, and either attack or observe, depending on their strength and numbers."

Hasek looked past Steiner's armoured car and saw the motley group of approaching panzers. "I flew the reconnaissance mission this morning. The British have a full squadron of their Crusader tanks, as well as armoured cars and a good number of desert scout vehicles, some of them portee-armed. Do you think you can handle them?"

"I am a Regiment Brandenburg officer," Steiner said lightly. "I can handle anything."

Once the panzer formation set up their leaguer at one end of the airfield, Hasek took Steiner and Kessler on a brief inspection of the installation. The garrison included a squad of ten infantry seconded to Hasek's command, led by a *Feldwebel*, stationed there as a security detail. In addition, there were ten other men, all *Luftwaffe*, whose job it was to handle the airfield's day-to-day operations. Hasek was the only pilot, for there was only one plane.

"When it became clear that all the excitement was taking place near the coast," Hasek explained, "the rest of the aircraft and most of the men were taken north. But it was decided that someone needed to stay down here, in case a flight over the deep desert was necessary."

"Not a very exciting posting, is it?" Steiner asked.

"No," Hasek replied. "But on the other hand, I'm not being shot at by Spitfires every day."

When Steiner inquired about the defences, Hasek showed him the three *sangars* positioned around the airfield. Two of the positions contained MG-34 machine guns, each mounted on a tall tripod and fitted with an anti-aircraft sight. The third *sangar* was larger, and contained a 20mm Flak 30 anti-aircraft cannon.

"Two MGs and a single-barrel autocannon," Kessler observed. "That's not a lot of protection against an air attack."

Hasek shrugged. "Like I said, we were left here as an afterthought. At least the Flak 30 can chase away those pitiful Tommy armoured cars."

"I wouldn't feel very comfortable with only those weapons and a score of men," Steiner said, joining in the discussion. "You aren't so far from the front lines as to be safeguarded from attack."

Hasek's face took on a mischievous countenance. "Ah, but you haven't seen every card in my hand, gentlemen. Follow me."

Hasek walked them over to a particularly large, rectangular tent in one corner of the airfield, near the makeshift "hangar" of camouflage netting the Storch lived within when not in use. The tent was dusty and draped with a large camouflage net, and Steiner's keen eyes noted there wasn't the usual path of tracks in the sandy ground coming in and out of the tent's entrance.

Hasek stepped up and unfastened the ties holding the tent closed. Pulling one of the flaps aside, he looked over his shoulder with a grin.

"Gentlemen, after you."

Steiner stepped forward and entered the gloom of the tent. Ahead and slightly above him, there was a large, shadowy object, and he reached up a hand and touched the round, smooth surface of what could only be a large calibre gun barrel. As his eyes adjusted to the darkness, Steiner began to make out the details of muzzle, recoil mechanism, and the massive expanse of flat armour plate making up the weapon's gun shield. He knew it could only be one thing.

"*Mein Gott*," he murmured. "You've got an eighty-eight."

"What?" Kessler said from outside the tent, incredulous. "Let me see."

The senior officer threw the tent flaps wide, letting in more light. The weapon was unmistakable: a Flak 36 anti-aircraft gun, capable of hurling an explosive shell high into the air, or a high-velocity anti-tank round downrange with sufficient power to kill any tank in their enemy's arsenal from thousands of metres away.

The two men turned and looked at Hasek.

"How...where did this come from?" Kessler asked.

Hasek grinned. "I told you, this airfield used to be more heavily manned. We had a battery of four eighty-eights stationed here for air defence. But when the other planes and the rest of the men were shifted north, the big guns were moved as well - all except this one. The half-track used to move it had taken damage a month prior in a strafing run, and chose a poor time for the engine to give up its ghost. There was no spare part to repair it, and no spare vehicles to tow the gun, so they left it here and told me it would eventually be retrieved."

"Apparently," Steiner said, "that never happened."

Hasek shook his head. "Weeks went by, and I reminded them several times when I radioed in my usual reports, but nothing ever came of my requests. I don't think Command wanted to bother wasting the resources to travel all this way and retrieve one gun. I even asked the resupply crews if they'd take it back with them, but no one wanted to bother since they'd not been ordered to do so in the first place, and they were worried towing the gun would slow them down."

"So eventually, you decided to keep it?" Kessler asked.

"I decided to hide it away from prying eyes," Hasek replied. "If the Tommies spotted it from the air, they might think we were more important than we are, and send someone to bomb us. This way, it is out of sight."

Steiner's eyes were adjusted to the darkness now, and he walked around the giant cannon, his eyes roaming over the pistons and gears of its mechanisms. Everything appeared in good working order.

"It is fully functional?" he asked.

Hasek nodded. "When we decided to keep it, we drilled for a few days, fired a crate of shells so we could gauge the fall of shot, get a feel for its mechanisms. The men might not be as good as a trained crew, but they can service the gun well enough."

"Do you have any anti-tank shells?" Kessler asked.

69

Hasek walk further back into the tent. The SdKfz half-track that'd originally been tasked with moving the Flak 36 was right behind the gun, still loaded with crates of ammunition. Steiner wondered if they'd set the tent up around the gun and tractor exactly where they'd sat when the tractor's engine had died.

Hasek climbed on the back of the SdKfz 7 and unclipped an electric torch from his belt, flicking the switch and shining the beam on the various crates of 88mm shells. The beam settled on several crates in the middle of the vehicle's cargo bed.

"Three crates of *Panzergranaten* anti-tank shells," he said. "We've fired a handful, but that's it. We have high-explosive for both ground attack and air defence as well."

Steiner looked at Kessler. "What do you think?"

The older officer stared up at the massive weapon for a long moment. Finally, he thumped the 88's gun shield with a clenched fist.

"If we are smart, and we are careful, this changes everything," Kessler said. "She can kill the Tommy cruisers at more than double the range of a Panzer III's cannon. But we only have one, and limited ammunition. It would be easy to get over-confident."

"Then we need a plan," Steiner replied. "And to form a plan, we need better intelligence."

"What do you have in mind?" Kessler asked.

Steiner turned to Hasek. "How soon can you get back into the air?"

"The Storch is fueled and ready," Hasek replied. "I can be in the air sixty seconds after I climb into the cockpit."

Steiner turned to Kessler and made a supplicating gesture with his hands. "I want to see the British with my own eyes. With your permission, *Major*?"

Kessler smiled and shook his head. "I'm certainly not getting into one of those kites. Be my guest, *Hauptmann*."

Ten minutes later, Steiner was in the rear seat of Hasek's Storch, as the aircraft lifted off from the desert and climbed into the air. Steiner had never flown in such a small plane before, and found the experience both exhilarating and terrifying at the same time. Every gust of wind buffeted the light plane, and Hasek constantly worked at the controls to keep them steady.

"The desert, it heats the air below us, which rises up and plays havoc with the plane's controls," Hasek explained.

Steiner nodded. He looked out the cockpit windows all around them, craning his neck to look in as many directions as possible.

"What do you do if we're spotted by enemy fighter planes?" he asked.

71

Hasek laughed. "Hope their machine guns kill us before we burn up or hit the ground. If I die, I want to be in the air."

"Not very reassuring!" Steiner replied. He glanced behind his seat, where he'd crammed a pack containing food, water bottles, a flare pistol and a box of cartridges, as well as a rifle. He'd originally thought it prudent to be prepared if they had to make an emergency landing, but Hasek's cavalier attitude made Steiner wonder if he was being too optimistic in gauging his chances of surviving any kind of calamity. He looked up at the small circular window above and behind his seat.

"Why did you remove the machine gun?" he asked.

"No point to it, really," Hasek answered without bothering to turn around. "Just extra weight, and we'd probably just shoot off our own tail. Besides, there's always the slim hope that if the Tommies see we're unarmed, they'll just force us down. If we shoot at them, they'll blow us out of the sky."

Steiner signed and tried to relax, giving in to the logic - however dubious - of Hasek's argument. Instead, he took his field glasses from where they hung around his neck, and spent some time peering out from the Storch's cockpit. From several kilometres up, the desert was, if anything, even more like the ocean; a vast, nearly featureless plain stretching away as far as the eye could see, to where the earth curved away along the horizon.

But as the flight went on, and Steiner studied the terrain more carefully, he began to notice the small differences, the creases and folds in the desert landscape, the low ridges and hills. Like any good field officer, he had an excellent eye for terrain, and soon Steiner began to imagine moving panzers and armoured cars across the ground below him, where he might set up anti-tank guns, or manoeuvre unseen by the enemy.

Before an idea formed completely in his mind, the thin column of smoke from the still-burning supply depot became obvious on the horizon, and Hasek steered the plane to take them in a wide circle around the depot. Several streams of tracers arched up from the ground and reached for them, but the Storch was too far away to be threatened, and the machine guns soon stopped firing.

Through his field glasses, Steiner saw the squadron of British tanks surrounding the depot. A lone tank sat several hundred metres away, probably knocked out in the attack, a cluster of antlike figures surrounding it. A wisp of smoke rose from a destroyed tank in the middle of the depot, likely an Italian M13/40, and there was a wrecked and smoking light truck about a hundred metres from the damaged British tank. While the squadron of tanks was clustered too closely together, the light trucks, as well as a half-dozen armoured cars - British and Italian - were spread out in a wide perimeter, well dispersed to protect from air attack.

"Their tank commander must be a fool," Steiner said. "Look how close together he's parked his squadron. If we had a flight of Heinkels, they'd be nothing but scrap metal."

In the seat in front of him, Hasek nodded. "They haven't moved since I made my first flight earlier this morning. I don't know why, because they fired at me once before. At least the light trucks - those are probably their desert patrol men - have enough sense to disperse themselves."

Steiner looked at his watch. "Alright, I've seen enough. Let's get back and get on the wireless. If the man commanding those tanks is this stupid, it is an opportunity we can't afford to pass up."

"You'll never get a flight of Heinkels sent out here, despite what we were just saying," Hasek said. "Not for a target that small. Command won't risk them."

Steiner reached down and pulled a map from his case, scanning it for friendly airfields. After a moment, his eyes narrowed, and he chuckled to himself.

"*Oberleutnant,*" Steiner said, looking at the cluster of tanks far below them, "what is the maximum combat radius of a Stuka dive bomber?"

EIGHT

The Italian Supply Depot
November 16th, 1030 Hours

"There's that bloody Storch again!" Tommy Lynch shouted to the other two members of his truck crew, both of whom were lounging in the shade of the Chevrolet while he stood watch.

"If Meade doesn't move his arse soon," Higgins replied from below, "we're going to get bombed into little bits of buzzard bait. Just you see."

Lynch shielded his eyes with his hand and looked up into the air at the German reconnaissance plane as it began to circle them at a safe distance. A couple of the nearest LRDG trucks began firing machine guns up at the plane, but the tracers fell well short, and after a few bursts, the men ceased fire.

"Lads, I'm going to see what's keeping us here, so I will," Lynch said. He caught up his Thompson and slung the weapon, the climbed down off the bed of the truck. "Higgins, you're on watch, boyo."

The other Commando let out a sigh and climbed up into the truck with a curse. Lynch began to walk back towards the depot, two hundred yards away. Although Meade apparently didn't think air attack was likely, Eldred, Clarke, and Moody weren't taking any chances, and they'd dispersed their vehicles in a wide pattern around the depot, keeping them from making a single close target.

Meade, however, didn't see a need to spread out his squadron. The fifteen undamaged Crusader tanks formed a tight circle, with perhaps only thirty yards between tanks. *Like a ring around a bloody bull's-eye*, Lynch thought. A flight of Heinkel bombers could swoop in, aiming for the depot, and their munitions would disperse enough to smash a good number of the lightly-armoured tanks in the process.

Lynch glanced across the desert to the one tank damaged in the attack. The Italian's shot had shattered the lead sprocket wheel and severed the tread. Worse, the impact had bent the fitting between wheel and chassis, so replacing the destroyed wheel wasn't even an option. The tank would require a carrier and repairs at a base, with the nearest being a couple hundred miles to the northeast. Meade was furious, of course; the loss of a tank so early in his mission was unacceptable to the Major. Lynch had seen him berating the tank's crew for the loss of their vehicle, completely ignoring both the fact that none of the men had been injured, and that the crew had possessed the wherewithal to fire back against their assailant moments after being immobilized.

Further on in the desert, a curl of smoke still rose from the wrecked Chevrolet truck. Lynch had helped collect the bodies of two Commandos killed in the wreck, while the third crew member, a Desert Group man, had died from his injuries an hour later. One other Commando had died in the attack, while another had been badly wounded. As Lynch approached the area of the depot where the British officers were convening, he heard Eldred arguing with Meade.

"The weather is good, and we're far from any enemy airbase known to possess fighters or attack aircraft," Eldred was saying as Lynch approached.

"I'm afraid it is simply out of the question," Meade replied. "Command isn't going to risk a flight all the way out here for one man. Not with the operation so near at hand. He's simply going to have to tough it out."

Trooper Hall, the Commandos' medic, was standing next to Eldred and clearly frustrated with Meade's decision.

"Beg your pardon, sir," Hall said, "but he can't tough out internal bleeding. He'll be dead in a day if we don't get him medical attention immediately, because there's nothing I can do for him here."

Meade looked exasperated. "Well, that is terribly unfortunate. But we've got a mission to accomplish, and casualties were, and always are, the price we pay in war. You'll just have to try and make him as comfortable as possible until he passes. We've got to hit that airfield tomorrow, and then move on to the next target the day after. That timetable is non-negotiable!"

Lynch had known Hall long enough to spot when the man was ready to cook off, and at that moment the medic was fit to be tied. But before Hall said something to get himself in trouble, Eldred interjected.

"Trooper, please, allow me to have a private word with the Major," Eldred said.

After a long moment, Hall nodded and walked away. Lynch busied himself with pretending to lace up his boots as he continued to listen in on the conversation.

"Sir, I understand your position," Eldred said, "but I ask that you reconsider. You're new to the field, and especially, new to these men. Both the Kiwis and my lads are top-notch troops, and that's in part because they're possessed of a keen fighting spirit, and a very strong morale. But if these lads get to grumbling amongst themselves, why, they'll lose the edge that makes them so bloody good at what they do, and we can't afford to have that happen. Not all the way out here, Major."

"Get to the point, William," Meade shot back.

"Sir, try to raise Command on the RT. Put in a request for a plane. If you do it, you're showing the lads you're thinking of their welfare, that you're looking out for them.

Part of our job as officers is to reassure these lads that someone cares, someone's taking care of their needs."

Meade bristled at Eldred's comment. "Captain, I'll not have you lecturing me on what conduct befits an officer! I've served for many years-"

"Sir, with respect, Bovington isn't a field command in wartime. I've been under fire nearly every year I've been in uniform. If you fight for these lads, they will fight for you. If you do not, morale will crumble, and this mission will fail. It is that simple."

For a few seconds, Lynch believed Meade would continue to refuse Eldred's suggestion, but finally the Major's posture softened just a little, his shoulders drooping slightly as he looked around conspiratorially.

"Alright Captain, I'll make the request. I am not completely ignorant of the fact that an officer must make a show of things now and then, for the benefit of the other ranks," Meade said in a low voice Lynch almost missed.

The major walked away towards the Italian's wireless tent and Lynch saw Eldred let out a visible sigh of relief. The Commando captain caught Lynch's eye as the Irishman finished pretending to tie his laces and stood up. Eldred walked over to him, and Lynch offered a salute that was quickly returned.

"Trouble with your laces, Corporal?" Eldred asked with a smirk.

"All sorted out now, Captain, so they are," Lynch replied.

Eldred glanced skyward, towards the circling Storch. "Like a buzzard, that one. Second time he's come back. The lads are ready and alert for an air attack?"

Lynch nodded. "Aye, sir. That they are."

"Good, that's good," Eldred said. He stood for a moment, clearly mulling something over. "Lieutenant Price tells me you're a good lad to have in a tough scrap."

"I try to do my part, so I do now, sir," Lynch replied.

"We are a very long way from any other friendlies, Corporal," Eldred continued. "And, we're walking a very thin line between success and failure. I need men who can keep their heads about them and get stuck in, when a lesser soldier might think it's time to leg it. Do you understand?"

"I think so," Lynch replied. "You don't have to worry about me, Captain. Me and the other lads, Price's lads I mean, we've been in some bloody tough spots. We won't let you down."

Eldred nodded. "Excellent. Now then, since you're done eavesdropping on officers' private conversations, get on back to your truck and prepare to move out within an hour."

"We're finally ready now?" Lynch asked. "Beg pardon, Captain, but the lads and I have been wondering, that we have. Seems we were burning a bit o' daylight."

"Major Meade was most distressed with the state of his damaged tank," Eldred replied. "He also wanted to interrogate the Italian commander and glean any...intelligence the man might have to offer. The process took considerable time, with very little to show for it, I'm afraid."

"What are we to do about the Eyeties, Captain?" Lynch asked.

"Well, we can't very well just shoot them, can we?" Eldred said lightly. "And we can't bring them along with us. However, Meade is adamant that we make sure his precious tank is salvaged, so he's going to leave the crew with it. We'll give them all Thompsons and make sure the Italians are unarmed, leave enough food and water for them all to rest comfortably until the recovery vehicle arrives. We'll leave one of the Italians' lorries as well, take the other with some petrol and ammunition, along with the armoured car that survived the attack. Not a bad bit of plunder, although I wish we hadn't lost so many lads. Next time I'll let Meade have his way and lead the bloody charge with his Crusaders. We're to hit a reconnaissance airfield some ways north of here at first light tomorrow morning. That shouldn't be quite so tough a nut to crack."

81

"I won't mind stepping aside and letting a bloody great big tank get shot at instead of me, to be sure," Lynch said.

"Wise lad," Eldred said with a smile. "Now, off you go, and spread the word that there's just enough time for a brew up. We're going to move out as soon as we hear from Command about that medical flight."

"Do you think they'll send a plane, sir?" Lynch asked hopefully.

Eldred shook his head. "No, they won't. But Meade had to make the request anyway."

"Oh, I see, sir. That poor bugger never had a chance, did he?" Lynch asked.

"I'm sorry, Corporal, but if we wanted to die of old age, we wouldn't have volunteered to join a Commando unit." And with that, Eldred turned and walked towards the wireless tent.

"Speak for your own bloody self," Lynch muttered, as he watched Eldred depart, while overhead, the Storch slowly buzzed away, heading north.

"Aye, off with you now," Lynch muttered. "Maybe you'll run out of petrol and drop out of the sky, do us all a favor. If not, we'll see you in the morning. Have a brew ready."

NINE

Twenty Miles North of the Depot
November 16th, 1230 Hours

Unfortunately for Lynch and the rest of Meadeforce, his hopes of the German plane crashing in the desert were for nought. Little more than an hour after their departure from the Italian supply depot, Lynch saw half a dozen specks appear in the air over the horizon to the north of them.

"Aircraft, dead ahead!" he shouted to Lawless and Higgins.

All around them, the other LRDG trucks were responding to the sight of the oncoming aircraft. The formation immediately began to spread out, pushing the distance between each vehicle to several hundred yards. Behind them, the Crusaders also began to shift, breaking up their more orderly formation and increasing their speed. Lynch cursed the lack of a radio on their truck, since this far apart there was no way for the trucks to communicate with one another.

"What do we do now?" Higgins shouted over the roar of the engine.

"Don't bloody well ask me!" Lawless replied. "I've never been strafed!"

Lynch racked back the bolt of the Vickers. "It's not bloody pleasant, I'll tell you that now! Get ready with that Lewis gun, and be patient! You have to wait until they pull out of their dive, that's when they're the slowest and easier to hit."

By now, the flight of six Stuka dive bombers was spreading out, each pilot looking for a choice target. The planes passed overhead, too high and too fast to be hit by machine gun fire. Lynch looked behind them as he heard the telltale change in engine noise as one of the dive bombers began its attack run. Through the haze of dust and sand thrown up by the formation's movement, Lynch saw first one, and then a second Stuka come around from behind the formation, rolling and diving near vertically at a target far to their rear. A sudden thought struck him.

"The lorries!" he exclaimed. "They're going for the petrol lorries!"

As Lynch voiced his warning, an enormous mushroom cloud of flame and black smoke boiled up into the air, the sound of the explosion reaching them a moment later. He'd seen explosions just like it a year and a half ago, as the British Expeditionary Force retreated across the length of France, harried the entire way by German forces. The dive-bombers would target fuel dumps and lorries, the pilots knowing a modern, mechanized army lived and died by its supply of petrol.

"We've got to turn around!" Lynch shouted at Higgins. "There's no one defending the lorries!"

"Are you out of your bloody mind, mate?" Lawless replied. "They'll knock us to pieces!"

"If someone doesn't fight them off, we'll all be stuck out here when the petrol in our tanks runs out!" Lynch shot back. "We'll be as good as dead!"

Lawless and Higgins exchanged resigned looks, and without another word, Higgins turned the wheel and swung the Chevrolet around, heading back the way they'd came. To the east, another explosion blew a geyser of sand and smoke up into the air, but there wasn't the signature fireball of a destroyed supply of petrol.

Looking to either side, Lynch saw he wasn't the only one to take action. Several other trucks were racing back through the dispersed formation, the machine gunners in each vehicle readying their weapons. They passed within a few feet of a Crusader tank, and the commander standing in the tank's open hatch shouted something at Lynch's truck while waving his hands in a warding gesture, but his words were lost in the roar of the Chevrolet's engine and the squealing of the Crusader's treads.

Ahead of them, two more Stukas rolled in on an attack run, and this time Lynch saw the streams of tracer fire pouring from their wing guns, flaying the sand with bullets. The tracers raced across the ground and hammered a speeding lorry, the driver desperately trying to zig-zag and avoid being hit. First one Stuka, then another strafed the defenceless vehicle, and as the second plane finished its run, the lorry detonated in a fireball, bits of burned metal and meat spinning through the air as black smoke churned upwards.

"Those bloody murderers!" Higgins cried, beating a fist against the truck's steering wheel. "Poor buggers couldn't even fight back!"

"We can't help them now," Lynch replied, "but we might make a difference for that lot to the north. Bring us about!"

Higgins swung the truck to the left and Lynch clung onto the Vickers' mount as the truck rocked on its suspension, a thick plume of dust flying behind the vehicle. Other trucks were now arriving at the rear of the formation, and Lynch saw tracers reaching up into the sky after a prowling Stuka. The German pilot deftly avoided the ground fire with a flick of his wing, rolling out of the way and straightening in time for a gun run against another LRDG truck dead ahead. Plumes of sand stitched across the ground, and only a desperate wrench of the steering wheel saved the truck from being ventilated by 7.92mm bullets.

The strafing run brought the Stuka's flight path very near Lynch's truck, and although the pilot fired at them, the tracers went well overhead, overshooting by dozens of yards. In response, Lynch swung up the Vickers and let loose a long burst. The Stuka was too close to jink out of the way, and Lynch saw the dive bomber pass right through his tracers, but the plane appeared undamaged when it flew overhead a second later. He muscled the heavy machine gun around and fired at the retreating tail of the Stuka, but the range was already too great.

"We need more firepower!" Lawless shouted, after seeing the dive-bomber depart unharmed.

The whine of another bombing attack reached Lynch's ears, and he searched the skies until he saw another Stuka plunging towards a petrol-carrying lorry several hundred yards to his left. Higgins spotted the attack run at the same time, and shifted gears, trying in vain to win a race against the diving airplane. Lynch and Lawless opened fire with their machine guns in a desperate attempt to hit the Stuka before it released its payload, but instead they watched, helpless, as a hundred-pound bomb detached itself from the wing hard-point and slammed into the lorry's bonnet. The bomb's detonation was immediately followed by the lorry's cargo of

87

petrol vanishing in a ball of smoke and flame. Higgins drove the Chevrolet past the flaming wreckage in the hopes of spotting a survivor who'd bailed out at the last moment, but there was nothing left; the lorry was barely recognizable as any kind of vehicle at all, and nothing of the crew was identifiable.

The last couple of petrol lorries were driving in haphazard patterns, as fast as their overtaxed engines were able to move them. Overhead, the Stukas began circling for the kill, like hawks preparing to pounce upon fear-stricken hares. The LRDG trucks raced towards the lorries, machine guns hammering tracers into the sky in the vain hopes of warding off the dive bombers. But the distances involved were too great, the planes too fast; any trucks providing cover fire for one vehicle were too far away to defend any other, with the end result that coverage over any one lorry was too light to be effective.

One after the other, the Stukas rolled in, machine guns blazing, air horns trumpeting their deadly call. Lynch flailed the air with bullets, doing his best to try and make contact with one of the dive-bombers, now plunging down upon the plundered Italian cargo lorry taken from the depot that morning. A second Chevrolet truck joined in the air defence, a total of four machine guns hurling dozens of rounds a second into the air above the lorry. The Stuka passed through the wall of lead just as a pair of bombs detached from its wings, and as the plane pulled out of its dive, black smoke began trickling from the plane's engine cowling. Lynch heard the misfiring of the Stuka's engine as something mechanical went terribly awry. Suddenly, the plane's manoeuvre faltered, and just as the bombs struck on either side of the lorry and reduced it to flaming wreckage, the dive-bomber's engine burst into flames and the plane arrowed into the desert, turning itself into a ball of fire and greasy black smoke.

Lynch would have cheered their kill, if it hadn't come at such a cost. Above them, the five remaining Stukas circled the formation for a minute. Four of them appeared completely unharmed, while the fifth trailed a thread of dark smoke. The planes were too high above the ground to be threatened by machine guns, and even the *boomboomboom* of Harry Nelson's Breda autocannon had no effect. After a couple of circlings, the wounded Stuka and a wingman peeled off and headed north, while the other three turned to the southeast.

"Bloody hell," Lawless cursed. "They're going after the depot!"

"They're going to make sure we can't return there and refuel," Lynch replied. "Methodical bastards, so they are."

In the wake of the air attack, Meadeforce ground to a halt. The major's precious armour remained spread out, but the faster Chevrolet trucks and the armoured cars converged, without any coordination, on the burning wreckage of the Italian lorry. Only one tank, Meade's own Crusader, joined the gathering of vehicles. Lynch reloaded the Vickers, then asked Lawless to man the weapon while he jumped down and approached where the officers were congregating. Lynch saw Price standing near his own truck, shoulders stooped, staring at the burning lorry nearby. As he approached his commanding officer, Lynch tried not to notice the blackening stick figures ablaze in the lorry's cab.

"Did we lose them all, Lieutenant?" Lynch asked.

Price slowly nodded. "I don't think they even tried for one of the tanks, Corporal. Those Jerry pilots were following specific orders."

"Knock out our supply of petrol and leave us stranded in the desert," Lynch said.

"That's right. And I fear that might be just what's happened." Price looked past Lynch, towards the corporal's truck.

"How many full cans of petrol do you have aboard your truck?" he asked Lynch.

"We've only taken fuel from the lorries thus far, saving our own stores for emergencies," Lynch replied. "Bloody fortunate of us, so it is."

"Perhaps, and perhaps not," Price said, and rubbed his chin as he glanced over to where Meade and Eldred were arguing again. Meade kept pointing at his tank, while Eldred repeatedly gestured towards the nearest Chevrolet.

"What's all that about now?" Lynch asked.

"I would imagine the major is insisting we sacrifice the stores of petrol on the trucks and armoured cars in order to keep his tanks mobile," Price replied.

Lynch stared open-mouthed at Price for a moment. "But, that'd mean we'd be stuck out here in the desert! It's not our bloody problem that his great big tanks drink petrol like a red-nosed bishop drinks ale!"

Price's eyebrows shot up, and he made an unobtrusive silencing motion with his hands. "Remember who you're talking about, Corporal. Major Meade is still in command of this operation."

"Some bloody operation," Lynch growled under his breath. "More like a Fred Karno's Army, if you ask me."

"Fred Karno's or not, we're going to continue on and hit that airfield in the morning. We have no choice but to continue forward, because we can't go back - we don't have enough petrol to reach a friendly base."

"And what if there's no petrol at the airfield?" Lynch asked. "Maybe they only have aviation-grade spirit."

Price shook his head. "They'll have something, I'm sure. Every installation out here in the deep desert is an oasis of sorts. They'll have petrol, although maybe not as much as we need."

"What about getting on their RT and requesting a relief column?"

Price gave Lynch a rueful smile. "On the eve of the largest offensive of the desert war? No, I think not. We're a handful of expendable men and vehicles, sent to poke Rommel in the backside so he doesn't notice the fist coming for his nose until it's too late. If we're lost to the desert, as long as we've played our part, we'd be a small price to pay for the strategic advantage."

"Well bugger me for a game of soldiers," Lynch cursed, and with a departing salute to Price, he returned to his vehicle.

The butcher's bill eventually made the rounds - a dozen men killed in the air attack, with all the lorries a complete loss. Thankfully, all the vehicles had been topped off before departing from the supply depot, so most were relatively well-provisioned. But everyone knew the Crusaders drank more heavily than the other vehicles, and while they had sufficient fuel to cover the thirty miles between them and the airfield, the endurance of Meadeforce beyond that target was dubious.

Before leaving the scene of the air attack, Lynch, Higgins, and Lawless brewed up a pot of char, adding plenty of sugar and milk to the strong tea. The comfort brought on by the ritual was sorely needed, and looking to the other vehicles of Meadeforce spread around the desert, Lynch saw the thin lines of smoke climbing up from other brews, as everyone used the time to have tea and even make a hot meal.

Higgins handed Lynch a tin plate with two slices of plundered Italian bread piled high with warmed bully beef. Lynch thanked his squadmate and ate slowly, washing down each bite with a sip of tea. His eyes moved between the sky above and the horizon ahead, and he felt taut and unsettled.

Lynch had volunteered for assignment to 3 Commando on the promise that he'd be making a strong contribution to the war effort. He had pictured himself crossing the channel in daring raids, creating havoc and causing the Nazis as much trouble as possible. All those months ago, when Lord Pembroke had spoken with him, the elderly gentleman had promised that Lynch and the men of his unit were a scalpel, a razor-sharp but delicate blade, to be used with skill and precision against carefully selected targets.

But out here, now, in the middle of the Libyan Desert, Lynch felt betrayed. Like Price had said, they were an expendable resource, men whose value lay only in pretending to pose a threat in order to hide a real one. The assignment could have been given to any of the countless infantry platoons in the 8th Army. It was only luck - bad luck to be sure - which had selected them for the mission out of geographical convenience, since they were already stationed at the Siwa oasis and without orders at the time.

Finishing his bread and bully beef, Lynch chased the meal with the last of his tea and scooped up a handful of sand, scouring clean his plate and cup. It was going to be a long war, and until it was over, he had little choice in the matter of assignments. The only thing left for him to do was perform his duties to the best of his ability, guard the backs of his mates, and kill as many Eyeties and Jerries as possible, so the war ended all the quicker.

Lynch heard the distant rumble of tank engines, and saw the rest of Meadeforce preparing to move out. By now, burial details had already attended to those men killed in the air attack, but thick black smoke still rose from the shattered wrecks of the lorries. The sight reminded Lynch all too well of the fall of France the year before.

Let's hope this caper turns out differently, he thought. *For all our bloody sakes.*

TEN

The Luftwaffe Reconnaissance Airfield
November 16th, 1700 Hours

Karl Steiner was in high spirits. Although initially disappointed that only a half-dozen Stuka dive-bombers were sent in answer to his request, their mission to destroy the British forces' supply vehicles was reported to be a complete success. With so few planes, Steiner had known there was no hope in destroying the armour itself; a direct hit with a bomb was necessary, and although a few tanks would have been destroyed, the action would have taken longer and with greater risk. But going after the soft-skinned transports was a much easier task. A bomb blast that merely sprayed shrapnel against the hull of a tank would rip apart a transport and its cargo with little difficulty, and while the Stuka's machine guns were useless against a Crusader tank or armoured car, they'd wreak havoc against a lighter vehicle.

In the desert, the last two years had emphasized to both sides the value of logistics, with the vast distances traveled and the demand the rough terrain placed on both men and machines. Steiner knew each of the transports destroyed was, in its own way, more costly a loss to the approaching British

95

than the destruction of a tank or armoured car. Kill one fighting vehicle, you only remove that one piece from the board. Kill a supply vehicle, and you have the potential to change the entire game.

And changing the game was Steiner's goal. Standing in the airfield's command tent with Kessler and Hasek, the three men pored over a hand-drawn map of the terrain around the airfield, sketched out by the *Luftwaffe* officer based on his observations while flying countless missions.

"I've taken my Kübelwagen out to this fold in the ground here," Hasek pointed to a line on the map a kilometre from the airfield. "It isn't much, but it is big enough to hide panzers."

"Even my Panzer IVs?" Kessler asked.

Hasek nodded. "Yes, although just barely. You'll have to be careful how you place them, but you will be able to stage them turret-down if you find the right spot. The rest won't be a problem."

"How will their howitzers compare against the British tank guns?" Steiner asked.

Kessler made a sour face. "Not as well as I'd like, but against the Tommy cruisers, even the HE shells will make quite a mess. Besides, the Panzer IIIs will be our primary tank-killers. If we're lucky enough to get flank shots within a thousand metres, we'll punch right through their armour."

"What about the towed guns?" Hasek asked them. "No offense to you gentlemen, but they don't look particularly impressive."

"It isn't the size of the shot that counts," Kessler replied, "It's the velocity and accuracy. Trust me, those Pak 36s are killers against light armour, especially if they have the advantage of surprise. Once they're dug in along here," Kessler pointed to a spot on the map, "they'll be almost impossible for the Tommies to see, at least until it's too late. A light anti-tank gun is far more difficult to spot than a panzer, even more so if it's not silhouetted against the horizon."

"And that leaves the eighty-eight," Steiner's finger tapped the airfield on the map. "Are you sure your men are capable of firing it effectively in combat?"

Hasek nodded. "As with the rest of the plan, surprise will be our greatest asset. If your ambush works, there will be enough confusion to give them quite an advantage early on, especially at great range. We'll be able to kill Tommies at more than three kilometres."

"We need to draw them in closer first," Steiner said. He placed his finger on the map. "Here should do it."

"They can cover that distance very quickly," Hasek warned, "especially their armoured cars and those desert trucks."

"What do you think?" Steiner asked Kessler.

The older officer studied the map for a long moment. "It will all depend on the man leading the armour. Those cruisers, the Tommies treat them like cavalry horses. They love to rush about the desert, making great sweeping flank attacks and other fancy manoeuvres, like they're out on a parade ground. The terrain here, to the west, will be more favorable."

"But do you think they'll press home the attack?" Hasek asked. "One hit from the eighty-eight, they'll know what they're facing."

Steiner smiled. "They have to attack, they have no choice."

Reaching over, Steiner picked up a large-scale map of the deep desert and unfolded it onto the table. His finger circled the area to the south-east of the airfield.

"There is almost nothing permanent in this area, especially after my own outpost was destroyed two weeks ago. Running into the supply depot yesterday was no accident. The British knew it was there and deliberately attacked and secured it. I think the same holds true for this airfield. Taking this installation and denying *DAK* Command your reconnaissance flights is just what they'd want to do before moving a large armoured force through the southern corridor."

Steiner drew his finger along a sweeping arc from the Egyptian desert near Siwa, into Libya and up towards Tobruk. He looked up at the two other officers. "I hate to admit it, but I think the generals were right to send us here."

Kessler let out an indeterminate grunt. "I am still not convinced. You only saw a squadron of tanks and some light vehicles. That's nothing. This could just be a reconnaissance in force, a probing manoeuvre to see what sorts of resources we have this far south."

Hasek waved his hands in a dismissive gesture. "Gentlemen, whatever it might be, we have to deal with the reality of an enemy force, larger than our own, most likely attacking us tomorrow morning. Now, you said they have no choice. What do you mean?"

"It is simple," Kessler replied before Steiner could speak up. "This airfield is the only installation close enough to reach with the fuel in their tanks. If it is a choice between pressing the attack and taking our fuel stores, or retreating back into the desert, only to run out of fuel and be left stranded, they'll attack."

"You're sure of this?" Hasek asked.

Kessler shrugged. "It is what I would do. And you, *Hauptmann*?"

"I would make the same decision," Steiner said. "Now, *Major*, with your permission, I'd like the *Oberleutnant* to take me up on one more reconnaissance flight. If the British are to strike at dawn, they'll have to leaguer close, most likely within a dozen kilometres or less."

Kessler nodded and looked to Hasek. "Is there enough daylight for a flight?"

Hasek checked his watch. "Yes, but we'll have to hurry. If we're not in the air soon, we'll have a devil of a time spotting them if they're staying dispersed until nightfall."

"Then it is settled," Kessler said. "I will make a last check of the preparations while you two are in the air. Then, when you return, a last briefing with the men, and a sleepless night before a dawn engagement none of us may live through. Another glorious battle for the heroes of the Third Reich!"

"*Heil Hitler!*" Hasek said, snapping out his arm in a salute.

Kessler smirked. "Oh yes, by all means."

It took a supreme effort of will to keep Steiner from laughing out loud as he followed the somewhat bemused *Oberleutnant* from the tent to the waiting Storch.

ELEVEN

Ten Miles South of the Airfield
November 16th, 1800 Hours

"You've got to be bloody joking!"

Lynch looked up from his bully beef and biscuits and looked in the direction Nelson was pointing. High above them, Lynch saw the now-familiar shape of the Storch, and his ears picked up the faint droning of its engine. The little plane was making a wide circle around their leaguer at an altitude too great for any of their weapons.

"Like a bleedin' vulture, so he is," Lynch muttered.

The two men were sitting with Lieutenant Price and the rest of their squad, having a hot meal cooked over a small sand-and-petrol fire before darkness came and no open flames would be permitted. Each man had a mug of hot, sweet tea fortified by a tot of rum or whiskey, as well as bully beef and biscuits, along with the last of the Italian cheese, sausage, and bread. Trooper Herring, proven to be one of the squad's best plunderers, had acquired a bottle of Italian red wine, and several of the lads were passing it back and forth, diminishing its contents rapidly.

"There's nothing to be done," Price said resignedly. "The Germans will now know we've not turned around, and they can only assume we'll be attacking in the morning."

"D'you think they've got anything we should worry about?" asked Higgins.

"Major Meade tells me early recce flights over this airfield showed an anti-air battery of eighty-eights, but the most recent observations indicated that the guns have been taken away, and the size of the installation much reduced. They may have some light weapons, but I can't imagine it's anything a squadron of tanks can't handle."

"So we're letting them armoured boys get shot at first?" Nelson asked.

Price nodded. "The Sabre squadron will lead the attack. We'll be splitting the trucks and armoured cars into two flanking elements, and while the armour takes the airfield, we'll swing around on both sides and button them up so no one scuttles away."

"Can't imagine any of the Jerries trying to scarper off," Lynch said. "Nothing around us for miles in any direction, we'd just follow along and wait for the buggers to break down."

"Regardless, Major Meade is highly concerned about the Germans flapping away with much-needed supplies. So, we'll do our jobs and make sure that doesn't happen," Price replied.

Overhead, the Storch's engine changed pitch, and the plane turned and flew off to the north, returning to its airfield. Everyone watched it go in silence for several minutes, until the plane disappeared from view.

Bowen, sitting to Lynch's right, watched the Storch depart through his field glasses. "Why do you suppose we've only been attacked by one flight of Stukas?" he wondered aloud.

"I don't know, and I don't bloody care," Lynch said to him. "I hate those bastards, so I do. Made the retreat to Dunkirk all the more bleedin' miserable."

"The RAF didn't have much problem with them," Herring said. "Can't imagine they were all that scary falling out of the sky in flames."

"Don't bloody talk about what you don't know," Nelson growled at Herring from across the circle of men. "You weren't there, so shut your gob."

"Or what?" Herring said flatly, staring at Nelson over the neck of the wine bottle raised to his lips.

"Or I'll get up and shove that bottle so far up yer arse, you'll be doing hand-stands to drink from it."

There was a moment of complete silence until first Herring, then Nelson, started to rise to their feet. Before either could make a hostile move, however, Price cleared his throat.

"Gentlemen, rather than someone being rudely violated with that bottle of red," Price said in a neutral tone, "I would like a sip if there's any left."

Herring and Nelson eyed each other like a pair of dogs challenging each other across a city street. Finally, without a word, Herring handed the wine bottle to Price.

"Thank you, Trooper. Most kind of you," Price said, before indelicately taking a slug of *vino* right from the bottle. He swished it about in his mouth before swallowing.

"Not bad," Price declared. "A bit sharp, but as this is the middle of the desert, I'm willing to be forgiving. Besides, my palate is a little rusty."

There was an uneasy chuckle from several of the men, and at last, with the tension somewhat alleviated, Herring and Nelson slowly sank back to their seats, all the while staring daggers at each other.

"Lieutenant," Lance Corporal White spoke up, "what d'you suppose is the next target, after the airfield?"

Price thought for a moment. "According to Meade's intelligence, there's another depot, much larger than the last, north of the airfield. The problem is, we don't have enough petrol for the tanks to reach it as it is right now. The Italian armoured cars and the Chevrolets might make the journey, though."

"So we'd what, leave the armour here?" White asked.

Price gave a small shrug. "That would be up to Major Meade to decide. But considering the timetable of the offensive, it might be more important to attack the depot with tanks and hope the defenders relay that information up the chain of command, to add confusion to the events of the eighteenth, when all the other tanks pour over the border far to the north. That is, after all, why we're here in the first place."

"Beggin' your pardon, sir," Johnson, Bowen's spotter, replied, "but if it's all the same to you, I'd rather be in Scotland right now."

The comment caused more than a few laughs from the circle of men, and what tension remained in the air quickly evaporated.

"I must say, I agree with your sentiment completely," Price answered. "It'll be good to get back to our homeland once more."

"Aye, and back to the training grounds," muttered Sergeant McTeague. He took his pipe from between his lips and pointed its stem at the men. "All ye sluggards are gettin' soft feet, swanning about the desert in these trucks. A few good day marches up and down some hills with a full load on your backs will make you proper soldiers again."

McTeague's comment was met with a chorus of groans that put a smile on the Scottish sergeant's lips. He stuck the stem of his pipe in his mouth and puffed triumphantly.

"Lieutenant, do you have any idea now, when we might return home?" Lynch asked.

Price shook his head. "I imagine if the powers-that-be behind the lines at Headquarters have no further use for us, we might be sent back by the end of the month. There was discussion of a possible mission to take place before the end of the year, and we may be home in time to take part, if it hasn't been scrapped for some reason."

"One battlefield after another," Trooper Hall said gloomily. "It's only going to get worse, before it gets better, isn't it?"

"The last we heard," Price said, "Jerry was giving the Soviets a good drubbing, pushing them back hard. I imagine things have slowed down with the winter, but if Stalin is forced to capitulate, the Germans will be able to turn their full attention on us."

"Not happy with Ivan's chances, to be sure," Lynch said. "The Finns gave 'em quite the bloody nose last winter, so they did."

"Aye, that may be true," McTeague replied. "But this time, the Ivans are the ones defending hearth an' home. If they're smart - and Stalin's a bloody clever bastard - they'll trade ground for time, draw the Jerries in deep, then the bear brings its jaws together, and chews up the Nazis."

"Let's hope so," Higgins said, staring into the bottom of his mug, "or we'll be fighting Jerries in the streets of London by this time next year."

"On that cheery note," Price said with finality, "I've got to meet with Major Meade and the other officers before catching a few hours of sleep. I suggest you lads get all the rest you can, because it's going to be an early morning."

"It's always an early morning," grumbled Johnson.

"As I said, sluggards all of ye," McTeague stood and stretched before picking up his Thompson. "Now, off with the lot of ye. Back to your trucks."

After a few moments of grousing, the Commandos got to their feet and gathered their weapons and kit. Lynch turned to Bowen. "Driving your truck tomorrow, Rhys?"

The Welshman nodded. "Not much use for my sniper rifle in a moving truck, and Johnson likes the Vickers."

"Well then, good luck now, and good hunting."

Bowen smiled. "You too, Tommy."

The two men shook hands, and Bowen walked off, his spotter by his side. Lynch watched his friend leave for a moment, then turned to Higgins, standing nearby.

"Alright now," Lynch said, stifling a yawn, "who gets first watch?"

TWELVE

Five Miles South of the Airfield
November 17th, 0600 Hours

Lieutenant Alan Chalmers stood in the open hatch of his Crusader tank and scanned the northern horizon for the twentieth time in as many minutes. His troop of three tanks was second from the right, Wilson's troop forming that flank, while to his left, Major Meade's headquarters troop of four tanks formed the centre of the formation.

The sabre squadron was moving north along a broad front, almost a mile wide, with a hundred yards between each tank in order to give them the best chances of spotting the target. Although their navigation so far left little to be concerned about, the vast, featureless desert meant they were taking no chances in locating the airfield. The morning air was cool, with only a slight breeze, and with the sun to his right, well out of his eyes, Chalmers felt the morning provided optimum conditions for their manoeuvres.

And it was a *manoeuvre*, not an attack, or a battle, he reasoned. There was little the Germans could field to defend a mere recce airfield that would give much grief to a squadron of fifteen cruiser tanks. Chalmers didn't discount the possibility of the defenders possessing a light AT-gun or two, but their tanks' Besa machine guns and the 3-inch howitzers of the two close-support tanks within the HQ troop would see to those in short order. In reality, Chalmers anticipated that the whole action would be over in a few minutes, with the expenditure of only a few dozen machine gun bullets to show the Jerries they meant business.

It would be the second combat action of his short career, the first being the attack on the supply depot the day before. Chalmers was fortunate enough to have fired a shot with his two-pounder and seen it hit, but the poor Eyetie tank had been riddled with shots and burning within moments, and there was still debate over which tank would claim the squadron's first kill of the war. Chalmers certainly hoped it wasn't the last, for he and the other troop leaders of the squadron had been incredibly disappointed when Meade was assigned this mission. Swanning about in the deep desert shooting up depots and airbases wasn't where the real glory was found. More than anything else, Chalmers wanted to pit his tank against the Germans, to go head to head against a Panzer III and knock a hole in it. A storied battle record would serve him well, making a promotion to squadron leader and eventually regimental commander much more likely. But none of that would be possible if he was stuck out here in the middle of nowhere.

Chalmers' headphones crackled as the RT came alive.

"Hello all stations GAMO," Meade's voice came through clearly, "this is GAMO calling. We are approaching the target point very shortly. Report immediately if you see anything. GAMO off."

Chalmers brought his field glasses up once more and peered ahead, bracing himself against the armoured hatch cover next to him. For perhaps a minute he saw nothing, before suddenly blinking at the faint hint of a hair-thin structure rising up into the air, far ahead of them. Chalmers took away his glasses for a moment and rubbed his eyes, then brought the glasses back up and looked again, making tiny adjustments to the focusing wheel. He convinced himself he was looking at the airfield's wireless tower.

"Calling GAMO, this is GAMO Three calling," Chalmers radioed in. "I see the tower, directly in front of me, approximate figures two zero zero zero yards distant."

"GAMO calling GAMO Three, good show. All stations GAMO, pull into close formation, and report in when you've made visual contact yourselves. GAMO to all stations BAGO, target sighted, begin your manoeuvre. GAMO off."

Soon, each of the three other troop commanders called in, reporting that they'd made visual contact with the airfield. By now, the tops of the larger tents were visible, and a small number of large vehicles, what appeared to be lorries, were seen nearby.

"Calling GAMO, this is BAGO One calling." Chalmers heard the voice of the armoured car squadron's commander, a captain named Moody. "There is a shallow ravine here to the east, running in a north-south direction. It looks like it might give us cover while we move up, over."

"BAGO One, go ahead and move into the ravine, just be sure you won't get boxed in at the end. Off to you."

Chalmers looked to the east and tried to spot the armoured cars and LRDG trucks, but the sun was barely over the horizon, and he didn't want to blind himself by squinting into it just before going into action. He turned back to look at the airfield again, just as a flash and a puff of smoke appeared from one of the larger tents, almost as if-

There was a *crack* and a buffet of air from his left, and Chalmers whipped his head around. He saw a plume of sand erupt two hundred yards behind them, and a few seconds later, the *boom* of a heavy gun reached his ears. Chalmers' mind raced, for the sound wasn't like that of an artillery piece or a light AT gun. Although he'd never heard one before, he could almost imagine it might have sounded like…

There was another flash and puff of smoke, and a second later, a horrific sound of high-velocity steel meeting an insufficient mass of armour plate. Chalmers saw chunks of metal flying into the air from the front of the second HQ Crusader, Lieutenant Sommersby's tank. Almost immediately, the tank burst into flames, smoke billowing out of every hatch, and the tank ground quickly to a halt, dropping out of formation. Chalmers could not help but look back in horrid fascination as an internal explosion rocked the dying tank, ripping away the turret and sending it toppling onto the sand.

"All stations GAMO, that was an eight-eight! I say again, that was an eight-eight!" Meade's voice cut through the headphones and shocked Chalmers back to the reality of the situation. "Turn west figures forty-five degrees immediately and move at best speed while we fire smoke. GAMO off."

"Driver," Chalmers spoke over the intercom, "turn forty-five degrees left, and increase to best speed."

"But sir," It was Miller, Chalmers' gunner. "We'll be exposing our flank to that great beast of a gun!"

"It's a bloody eighty-eight, you fool," Chalmers shot back. "It won't matter where it hits us."

The tank shuddered for a moment as the driver worked the track clutches, and their course shifted to put the airfield off to their forward right flank. There was another flash, and a moment later, sand geysered up into the air between his trailing tank and the lead tank of Wilson's troop. Another round followed soon after, passing between Wilson's tank and the lead tank of his troop.

There were two *thumps* from ahead of his tank, and Chalmers turned to see puffs of smoke curling away from the two close support Crusaders. Each of the tanks was fitted with a three-inch light howitzer, and most of their shells were smoke rounds, used to cover the advances and retreats of the squadron. Two gouts of white smoke popped into the air a hundred yards short of the 88, followed soon by two more. The gunners were being clever, trying to get the smoke as close to the enemy as possible, so it would afford the squadron the most protection.

But even as a third pair of smoke shells landed, the eighty-eight fired again, the lethal shot so low Chalmers thought he saw a trail of dust raised from the ground in the wake of its passing. Again, the shell missed Wilson's lead tank by mere feet, and Chalmers found himself urging the tank's driver to push his mount to the limit. He could only imagine the dread of the tank's crew, knowing the eighty-eight's gunner was singling them out for destruction.

A moment later, that destruction came to pass. The armour-piercing round struck the Crusader broadside, and Chalmers looked on in astonishment as he saw the shot pass right through the tank, blowing out the other side in a spray of hull fragments. The tank's commander, standing in the open hatch, let out a brief shriek before disappearing in a gout of flame and smoke. A heartbeat later, the tank simply exploded into a ball of fire and spinning chunks of armour.

Enough was bloody well enough, Chalmers thought. It was time to fight back. He gauged the range between his tank and the airfield to be about fifteen hundred yards. Beyond what he'd consider maximum effective range of his tank's machine gun, but Chalmers knew the weapon was lethal far beyond that distance.

"Gunner, MG, anti-tank gun, western end of the airfield, fifteen hundred yards," Chalmers ordered over the intercom.

The turret whined as Miller rotated it to the right, bringing the tank's co-axial Besa machine gun onto the target.

"I have it, sir. Extreme range, though," Miller answered.

"I know! Gunner, fire!" Chalmers replied.

A stream of tracers arced up into the air, descending with deceptive slowness towards the airfield. Chalmers watched them vanish into the sand, a few of them bouncing off rocks and ricocheting back up into the air.

"Gunner, you're short. Increase range two hundred yards and fire," Chalmers ordered.

Miller fired another long burst from the Besa MG, and this time Chalmers saw the tracers float down into the middle of the tents around the western end of the airfield.

Having found the range, Chalmers keyed the radio mic. "GAMO Three to GAMO Three A and B, engage enemy eighty-eight with your machine guns, range is figures one seven zero zero yards. GAMO Three off."

The turrets of the two tanks on either side of him rotated, and soon, all three of his troops' machine guns were firing bursts in long arcs towards the tent concealing the eighty-eight. For a few seconds, the deadly gun went silent, and Chalmers congratulated himself on his quick thinking.

"GAMO to GAMO Three, I did not give the order to fire! We need to take any petrol stores intact! If those tracers ignite that fuel, we're done for! Cease fire!"

Bloody Meade! Chalmers gritted his teeth. Both of his troop tanks stopped firing the moment their commanders heard Meade's order, not waiting for him to relay it on.

"Sir?" Miller asked from inside the turret.

"Gunner, cease fire, but make sure that Besa is loaded and ready," he replied.

The eighty-eight, sensing its reprieve, fired again. The shot passed behind the last tank in Wilson's troop, kicking up a gout of sand a hundred yards to the south-west. Looking ahead, Chalmers saw the CS tanks had laid down more smoke, and within a few moments, if they were lucky, they'd be in a position where the smoke cloud obscured them from the eighty-eight.

Suddenly Chalmers heard what sounded like the flat *cracks* of high-velocity tank guns, coming from the north-west. He raised his field glasses, trying to see who the leading tanks might be shooting at, when he saw the lead tank of the first troop grind to a halt and begin to burn. Immediately, streams of tracer fire began to arc out from the other two tanks in the troop, scything across what at first appeared to Chalmers to be open ground.

"All stations GAMO, this is GAMO One calling. Anti-tank gun screen to our front, figures six zero zero yards. My sergeant's tank is dead, we are attempting to suppress with our MGs, over."

"GAMO calling GAMO One, do you have figures on number of guns, over?" Meade replied.

"GAMO One here, we count at least, repeat, at least figures four guns, well dug in, over."

"GAMO calling BAGO Two, move with all haste to engage the anti-tank gun screen ahead of us. Off to you. All stations GAMO, continue current course. We need to get behind that smoke screen before doing anything else. Off to you. BAGO One, how close are you to the airfield, over?"

"BAGO One calling GAMO," Moody replied. "We are still in cover, now figures one two zero zero yards from the airfield. Will emerge as close as possible and engage the-"

Chalmers heard the muffled *clang* of steel plate breaking under impact and a cry of pain directed straight into the live microphone.

"Panzers! Bloody panzers! All stations, it's a trap! The ravine is filled with-"

The air was filled with static for a moment before the transmission went dead.

Chalmers turned to the east and squinted into the sun, raising up his field glasses and scanning the terrain. A thin column of black smoke began to climb up into the air some two thousand yards away.

"GAMO calling any stations BAGO One, report!" Meade's voice cut through the net, a note of rising panic in his voice.

"The captain's 'ad it!" a voice cried over the radio. "There's panzers hiding in here, it's a bloody ambush!"

The sound of an autocannon firing came over the radio, and pulling one earpiece away from his head, Chalmers heard the weapon firing off in the distance, the *boomboomboom* of an Autoblinda's cannon. There were a pair of louder, flatter-sounding shots a moment later, and a ball of fire rose up out of the ravine. The open channel squealed in sharp static for a second before going dead again.

"GAMO calling any stations BAGO One, pull back and get clear. Off to you. All stations GAMO, move to a position behind the smoke screen. GAMO One and Two, suppress the AT gun screen with your MGs. Off to you. GAMO Three and Four, turn and engage any enemy armour appearing from the east. Off to you. BAGO Two, deal with that AT gun screen, then move at best speed to try and neutralize the eighty-eight. We need to deal with it before we can fight the panzers. Off to you."

Chalmers saw the two CS tanks firing as fast as their gunners and loaders could work their howitzers, the shells creating a thin but possibly life-saving cloud of concealing smoke. He hoped it would make the difference, but a pair of three-inch guns was woefully inadequate for the task at hand. When cruisers went into battle behind a screen of smoke, they were usually supported by a battery or two of twenty-five pound guns hurling massive smoke shells.

With the eighty-eight to their right, an enemy gun screen ahead, and now panzers to the rear, Chalmers suddenly felt very, very alone.

"Driver, wheel right, bring us about facing to the east. Loader, two-pounder, load and make ready additional rounds. Gunner, two-pounder, prepare to engage enemy armour, current estimated range two thousand yards."

Well, you wanted some real action, Chalmers scolded himself. *Let's hope we live through it.*

THIRTEEN

West of the Airfield
November 17th, 0615 Hours

Lynch didn't know exactly what was going on, but he knew it couldn't be good. The sounds of large-bore cannons firing, as well as the chatter of machine guns and the higher-pitched sounds of light, high-velocity tank guns were coming from the east, and smoke columns were climbing up into the air. The pair of Autoblindas and the single Morris car ahead of them had suddenly changed direction, their course now almost due east, towards the airfield. Because the trucks lacked the radios carried aboard the armoured cars, their orders were to simply follow behind their bigger kin in a form of "follow the leader" and engage where indicated.

As they approached the airfield, the situation became clear. Directly to the east, the airfield sat behind a slowly-drifting smoke screen, the two CS Crusader tanks firing shell after shell as fast as their guns could be loaded. The rest of the sabre squadron, or what was left of it, was split into two groups: those engaging a line of anti-tank guns to the north-west, and those turning to face a dozen or so dots to the south-east. The dots moved in a way that was chillingly

119

familiar to Lynch, and brought to mind the battle of Arras, where he watched German panzers advancing past the shattered wrecks of Matilda tanks torn apart by eighty-eights. Watching those dots approach now, Lynch knew they could only be enemy armour.

As they approached the anti-tank gun line, the Autoblindas opened fire with their 20mm autocannons and machine guns. The turret-mounted Bren of the Morris car added its meagre firepower to the assault, and soon the gunners aboard the Chevrolet trucks opened fire as well. A storm of lead and explosive cannon shells sent a cloud of sand and pulverized rock into the air around the nearest Pak 36 guns, but the Germans had placed them extremely carefully. The gun carriages were situated in shallow depressions dug into the rocky ground, and the crews worked the guns from foxholes, providing them increased cover. In addition, the guns were spaced a hundred yards apart, deployed on a wide front and forcing the British to engage them not as a target *en masse*, but one tiny, well-protected emplacement at a time.

And the Germans weren't defenceless, either. An MG-34 team dug in behind and between the middle two Pak guns opened fire on the approaching British vehicles, forcing the Autoblindas to button up and the LRDG trucks to take evasive manoeuvres. The pressure off them for a moment, the nearest Pak gun crew moved to re-sight their gun towards the new threat. With a loud *clang*, an armour-piercing shell grazed the side armour of the lead Autoblinda and plowed a furrow into the desert sand. In response, the car's 20mm autocannon chattered, sending a half-dozen shells hammering into the gun emplacement. Lynch watched from a distance as the Pak 36's gun shield came apart in a spectacular display of flying metal and dust.

"Those Jerry blighters are done for!" Higgins shouted above the roar of the column's weapons.

As if in response, the MG crew chose that moment to rake their car with bullets. The sun compass next to the driver's seat was smashed into fragments, and a pack hanging from the side of the truck exploded into tatters and bits of shredded gear as it caught several slugs. Lawless let out a long string of curses.

"Are you hit?" Lynch shouted at the New Zealander.

"No, that was my bloody kit they just shot up!" Lawless replied. "Higgins, keep your bloody gob shut, mate!"

No sooner had the MG team attacked Lynch's truck than both Autoblindas, virtually immune to the weapon's fire, turned their autocannons on the German's slit trench. Each car fired off a twelve-round clip of 20mm high-explosive shells, and when the smoke cleared, all that was left of the gunners was the twisted wreck of a machine gun and a few scattered, bloody remnants of cloth and flesh.

Moments later, the armoured cars and LRDG trucks drove past the remains of the first Pak gun team and closed in on the second. The Pak crew tried to bring their gun around, but it was too little, too late. Lynch swung the Vickers MG towards their position, and with deliberate care, sprayed the gun and its crew with several tight bursts. One of the Germans attempted to return fire with an MP-40, but by exposing himself enough to fire the weapon, he caught a pair of .303 calibre bullets in the face, dropping him limp and lifeless back into his foxhole. As the truck sped past, Lawless threw a Mills Bomb at the emplacement for good measure. The blast ripped into a box of 37mm shells, and soon, the emplacement was engulfed in smoke and flame as the anti-tank rounds detonated one after another in a rapid-fire chain reaction.

With half their number wiped out, a column of fast-moving vehicles spitting machine gun fire coming from one direction, and several Crusader tanks firing their own MGs from another, the remaining Pak gunners clearly felt that seeking cover and surviving was preferable to manning their guns until the bitter end. Both crews disappeared into their foxholes, and Lynch saw a rifle tossed onto the ground from inside a foxhole next to the nearest gun. The vehicle column began to turn, coming to bear on the airfield hundreds of yards away.

In the distance, Lynch's eyes caught movement near the German lorries parked along one end of the airfield. A troop of four armoured vehicles of various types pulled out from behind the lorries, and before Lynch could say anything to Lawless or Higgins, the enemy column opened fire. 20mm cannon shells and machine gun bullets hammered across the leading armoured cars, and in spectacular fashion, the lead Autoblinda blew apart, its steel plate penetrated a dozen times by high-explosive and armour-piercing cannon fire.

"Bloody hell!" Lawless shouted. "We've been sandbagged!"

No sooner had the New Zealander spoken up, than the Morris car was ripped apart by the enemy's combined weight of fire. Even more lightly armoured than the Italian cars, the Morris was literally torn to pieces, plates of steel armour and mechanical innards flung yards in every direction. Lynch caught a glimpse of a severed arm cartwheeling in the air before it was hit by a stray cannon round and blown to gibbets.

The remaining Autoblinda gunned its engine in reverse, and returned fire with its own 20mm cannon. Its target, which Lynch realized was actually a Panzer II, soon ground to a halt as its thin armour succumbing to the same punishment it had dealt out only moments before. Soon smoke curled out of the panzer's hatch, and the vehicle shuddered to a halt, left behind as the three other vehicles - two light, four-wheeled cars and a heavy eight-wheeled model - rushed into battle, their cannons blazing.

The outcome was inevitable. The side hatches of the last Autoblinda popped open and a pair of figures tumbled out, followed by a gout of vile-looking black smoke. Even from a distance, Lynch identified one of the men as Captain Eldred.

"Higgins, bring us in behind the last car!" Lynch shouted. "We've got to fetch the captain before he's thrown in the bag!"

Indeed, the armoured cars continued to close in, but without their previous vigor, and their guns were silent. Lynch imagined the Germans, having knocked out the armoured cars, were expecting to scoop up the much more poorly armed LRDG vehicles.

However, not everyone was in agreement as to the state of the trucks' helplessness. From his right, Lynch heard the *boomboomboom* of a Breda autocannon, and he turned to see Harry Nelson's truck racing away at an angle, the muzzle of the portee-mounted cannon poking out over the left fender. Nelson's face was contorted in rage, and although he couldn't hear him, Lynch saw his squadmate was screaming at the top of his lungs, no doubt letting loose with a stream of profanity strong enough to curdle milk.

"What's that blinkered idiot doing?" Higgins cried. "He's going to get himself killed!"

"Nothing to be done about that madness now," Lynch replied. "Let's get in there and rescue the captain!"

Just then, Lieutenant Price's truck pulled alongside, and the lieutenant leaned out towards Lynch's car. "We've got to leg it!" Price shouted. "This whole operation's bungled! Meade's lot are brewing up like pots in a tea shop, and the rest of our men are dead or captured! Follow me!"

"I'm going in to pick up Captain Eldred!" Lynch shouted back.

Price looked towards Eldred, huddled behind the smoking wreck of his armoured car, a pistol in hand. He nodded.

"Alright, but be quick about it! We've got to salvage something from this disaster!"

With that, Price pulled away and headed west, followed by McTeague, whose truck carried the only remaining heavy weapon, the portee-mounted "squeeze bore" anti-tank gun. Lynch caught the sergeant's eye, and the Scotsman nodded to him once, then turned to say something to Trooper Hall in the driver's seat.

Lynch looked to the right and saw Nelson's truck still intact, racing across the desert at top speed. The 20mm Breda continued to fire, and Lynch saw enemy tracers from autocannons and machine guns whipping all around the vehicle. He knew without a doubt his friend's life was now measured in seconds, and he'd not waste the sacrifice.

"Go on now!" Lynch shouted to Higgins. "Move up to the bloody car!"

Higgins shook his head in disbelief, but moved forward nonetheless, keeping the smoking wreck of the Autoblinda between them and the advancing Germans. As they pulled up next to Eldred, Lynch leaned out and offered the Captain his hand.

"Up with ye now, sir!" Lynch shouted.

Eldred gave a last look at the man who bailed out with him, now crumpled in a heap against the rear wheel of the car. Lynch saw the man wasn't a Commando, but one of the armoured car crewmen from the 11th Hussars.

"Poor fellow just expired," Eldred murmured. "Didn't even get a chance to know his Christian name."

"Sir!" Lynch repeated. "Nelson's drawing their fire, but when they're done with him, we're sure to be next!"

Eldred's lips drew together in a tight line, and he gave the dead man next to him one last look before he tucked his .45 automatic back in its holster. Pulling a Mills Bomb from his belt, Eldred armed the grenade and tossed it into the open hatch of the Autoblinda, then took Lynch's arm and climbed aboard.

"Higgins!" Lynch shouted.

Without a second's pause, Higgins gunned the engine and the truck sped away, the Autoblinda blowing up moments later as the grenade detonated and set off the stored cannon shells and machine gun ammunition. A thick cloud of black smoke billowed from the wreckage, helping to conceal their departure.

Lynch looked back behind them, and through the smoke and flames, saw the three German armoured cars drawing close to what remained of Nelson's truck, now a tangled, smoking wreck sitting alone in the desert. Beyond it, off to the south-east, Meade's Crusaders traded shots with their main guns against the German panzers.

FOURTEEN

"Gunner, two-pounder, target is a Panzer III, dead ahead, range nine hundred yards. Fire!"

A second later, Chalmers was buffeted by the muzzle blast from his Crusader's main gun. The high-velocity shot arced through the air, and he used his field glasses to watch the round's trajectory, squinting against the morning sun to keep the tracer at the base of the armour-piercing projectile in sight. The round struck the turret of the panzer and ricocheted away.

"Hit, but failed to penetrate! Fire again!"

Through the body of the tank, Chalmers felt the breech snap closed as the loader rammed home another shell. The cannon bucked again, and this time Chalmers saw the round hit without bouncing off.

"Hit! Gunner, same target, keep firing as fast as you're able!"

The panzer, undaunted, continued to close the distance between them, and a moment later, its own cannon fired.

Chalmers didn't see the shot, but he felt the air swirl as the 50mm round passed him.

Chalmers fought the urge to flinch. *No sense in fearing those*, he thought to himself. *If you're hit, you'll never even feel it, so why worry?*

Looking across the battlefield at the remnants of the Sabre squadron, Chalmers realized there were far worse ways to die. Ahead of him, Wilson's tank was burning fiercely, and he knew he'd heard the man screaming from the tank's open turret hatch as the tank caught fire and began to burn. None of the crew had escaped, the four men incinerated, trapped inside a superheated steel box. Just one hit from a Panzer III's gun at a thousand yards had sealed their fate.

The last tank in Wilson's troop had turned to face the panzers. It was backing up slowly, firing as it retreated towards Chalmers' troop, engaging what appeared, unbelievably, to be another Crusader tank, painted in the same colours as the rest of the panzers. Chalmers could only imagine it was a captured tank, pressed into service. Behind and to the left of the captured Crusader, an even older captured A13 cruiser burned, Wilson's only kill before his own tank brewed up.

"GAMO calling all stations GAMO. Fall back in an orderly fashion, keeping your frontal armour towards the panzers. We shall make a fighting withdrawal to the south-west until we are out of range of the eighty-eight, off."

"Driver, reverse gear, as fast as you are able," Chalmers ordered. "Gunner, keep on that Panzer III until he brews up."

Their target panzer fired again, and the Crusader vibrated with the impact of the hit somewhere on the tank's right flank. Fearing they'd lost a track, Chalmers glanced over the side of the turret and saw half of the track guard had been ripped away. As the track moved, it made a terrible grinding noise against the twisted metal of the ruined guard, but it appeared intact.

That panzer's damage to their Crusader would be its last. Chalmers' gunner scored another hit, and with the target some two hundred yards closer, the shorter range paid off. The Panzer III came to a halt, the crew bailing out as smoke began to leak from the open turret.

"Gunner, good show!" Chalmers exclaimed. "Now, two-pounder, new target, Panzer IV to the left one hundred yards, range eight hundred yards. Fire when loaded."

Looking over the approaching enemy, Chalmers counted five Panzer IIIs and two of the larger IVs. Only one other III had been killed, hammered to death by the survivors of the two troops at the other end of their column. Meade's tank traded shots with another III, while the two IVs lobbed high-explosive shells at them from their low-velocity 75mm cannons.

Chalmers' gunner missed with his first shot, but the second struck home, the round spinning away through the air.

"Gunner, hit, keep at him!" Chalmers called into his intercom.

Lifting his field glasses, Chalmers scanned the horizon to the north-east, seeing a number of smoke columns in the direction of the Pak gun line. He saw what looked like several armoured cars burning, as well as others - German by their silhouettes - in motion. Although a two-pounder would make short work of the lightly-armoured cars, none of the remaining Crusaders could spare the time to engage, and it looked like the Germans were merely examining their handiwork after wiping out BAGO Two, the recce element sent out along that flank.

Chalmers felt his stomach clench with fear, and he fought the urge to be violently sick. Meade had led them into what was clearly a well-constructed trap, with a hidden eighty-eight, a line of Pak guns along one flank, and a squadron of hidden panzers along the other. If they'd swung right first, towards the ravine, they'd have run smack into the panzer ambush.

We never had a bloody chance, did we? Chalmers wondered.

A *clang* of metal against the side of the turret brought Chalmers back to the situation at hand. One of the Panzer IIIs had taken a shot at them, defending the Panzer IV they'd been targeting. The larger tank was now immobilized, a track shot away, and Chalmers' gunner was doing his damndest to kill it.

"Gunner, leave the Panzer IV be. Engage Panzer III two hundred yards to the right, range six hundred yards."

With a hellacious explosion, one of the two close-support Crusaders blew apart, the tank's turret pirouetting through the air. Chalmers saw the tank's commander spin away from the turret missing both his legs. In response, the other CS tank fired a three-inch HE round at its brother's killer, the high-explosive shell detonating right in front of the Panzer III. Unfazed, the panzer fired back, and was soon joined by another III. In seconds, the CS tank was hit multiple times, and Chalmers saw three of the crew bail out before the tank began to brew up. The three men huddled a few feet behind their dying tank, afraid of running away for fear of being cut down by the Germans, but knowing their tank was moments from blowing itself to pieces.

Chalmers made his decision. "Driver, pivot right. We're going to try and pick up Sergeant Dobson's crew."

The tank lurched under his feet and began to pivot. "Driver, cease pivot, continue reverse."

The move must have attracted the attention of the Germans, for the fire coming their way increased dramatically. A 50mm round tore away the right-hand turret hatch a foot from him, leaving Chalmers miraculously unharmed. Another round skipped across the side of the hull, leaving a foot-long groove of gleaming metal.

Chalmers made a quick inventory of the Sabre squadron. Both of the tanks in his troop were knocked out, and only his tank and Wilson's corporal were still in the fight on the right flank, Meade's tank was the only remaining tank of the HQ troop. Off along the left flank, he saw two Crusaders still firing. Out of the fifteen tanks operational twenty minutes ago, only five were left. The Germans still had - Chalmers scanned their lines with his field glasses - four Panzer IIIs, one IV immobilized, one still in the fight. The captured Crusader and another Panzer III were sending columns of black smoke billowing into the sky.

A second later, a shot from Wilson's corporal's tank struck the Panzer III firing on Chalmers in the turret, and the panzer went silent. Seconds passed and there was no fire, although the tank ground to a halt. A lone figure belly-crawled out of the panzer's turret hatch, and over the back of the turret. Chalmers wondered if it was the driver, and if that one shot had killed the rest of the crew.

"GAMO calling all stations GAMO." Meade's voice came over the radio. "We've evened the numbers, lads. Aim true, and we may just see our way clear of-"

The eighty-eight's armour-piercing shell ripped the turret clean away from Major Meade's tank. As Chalmers watched, mouth agape, another shell struck the crippled tank, this one smashing home right at the point of the tank's bow. The driver's compartment was pulverized, the front of the tank looking as if struck by a titan's warhammer. The third shell was high-explosive, and reduced the tank to little more than a circle of twisted wreckage a dozen yards in diameter.

Chalmers blinked a few times, unsure of what to do. He saw now that, with the approach of the panzers, the close support tank commanders had become distracted, and the smoke cloud - their only defence against that monstrous gun - had dissipated to the point where it was no longer effective. The eighty-eight's crew had no doubt been waiting for just such an opportunity, and ripped the centre tank from the squadron the moment they had a clear line of sight at a range of less than two thousand yards.

There was only one hope remaining. "All stations GAMO, this is GAMO Three calling. Engage the eighty-eight and reverse at all speed. Use your two-pounders. It's our only hope. Off."

"Gunner, two-pounder, new target. Eighty-eight, end of the airfield, range two thousand yards. You'll have to pitch them in high, but with luck we'll score a telling hit."

The tank's turret traversed slightly, and the tank rocked back as the main gun fired. Chalmers watched the fall of shot through his field glasses.

"Gunner, miss. Increase range one hundred yards and fire."

The two-pounder fired a moment later, and Chalmers saw the tracer disappear into the large tent covering the German gun. Immediately after, he saw tracers arcing in from the other three surviving tanks. Through it all, the eighty-eight remained silent.

Chalmers thumped his fist against the tank turret in triumph. He ducked his head down into the inside of the turret.

"Brilliant shooting, Miller! I think we got them!"

The Crusader rang like an immense bell as it was struck on the forward glacis, and Chalmers fell back into the turret, feeling sand and grit and bits of metal raining down on him through the open hatch above. He was momentarily deafened from the explosion, but he sensed the screaming of a man in terrible agony, and saw light streaming in through a gaping wound in the forward hull, where the driver's compartment would have been, if a shell hadn't opened the forward hull like a tin of beans.

Chalmers' vision swam, and he tried and failed to gain his footing, blinking away grit from his eyes. Miller's face appeared before him, streaked with blood, although Miller seemed alert and unharmed.

"Sir, are you okay?" Miller asked. "Bob's had it, blown to bits, and Alfie's a right bloody mess, near to cut in half, sir."

Chalmers swallowed, his throat achingly dry. He wondered for a moment what must have happened, and came to the realization they had been hit by an HE shell from one of the Panzer IVs.

"Bail out," he croaked. "Grab the Bren and the ammunition."

Miller hesitated for a moment. "Alfie, sir?"

Chalmers raised a shaking hand towards the turret hatch. "Go on, grab the Bren and out with you. I'll see to Alfie."

Miller nodded. The gunner reached for the Bren machine gun clipped to the inside of the turret and pulled it free, then took a moment to stuff several magazines into his jacket pockets before climbing out of the turret.

On hands and knees, Chalmers moved to where Alfie lay. The loader had been struck by a large piece of steel plate, and the jagged metal had torn clean through the man right above the belt. Alfie had blood running down his chin, and he twitched and spasmed as his hands reflexively sought to pull the steel plate free despite lacking any strength to do so. Alfie's eyes rolled towards Chalmers.

"M-made a g-g-good run of it, eh L-lieutenant?" Alfie whispered.

Chalmers nodded. "Cracking good crew, you lads. The best in the regiment."

"G-go on now, sir," Alfie said. "She could b-brew up any second."

"I can't very well leave you here, wouldn't be proper," Chalmers said.

Alfie shook his head, and his hand fumbled at his pistol holster. "I'll be a-alright, sir. Off with you now."

Unsure of what to say, Chalmers patted Alfie on the shoulder, then stood up, unclipping the Thompson from its place on the turret and grabbing a few spare magazines before climbing out of the tank. Outside, Miller crouched behind the Crusader's engine, Bren at the ready.

"Alfie?" Miller asked.

Before Chalmers could answer, there was a single pistol shot from inside the tank. Miller closed his eyes and whispered a curse.

Looking around, Chalmers saw the squadron was no more. In the time since they'd been hit, Wilson's corporal's tank had been knocked out and was now burning. A single crew member huddled in the sand, trying to keep a safe distance from the flaming vehicle. Off to the left flank, Chalmers saw the second CS tank had finally brewed up, the crew now crawling away from it as fast as they could, while keeping their dead tank between themselves and the Germans. Further on, Chalmers saw the last two Crusaders were also burning, one of them in such a terrible state that he knew they hadn't knocked the eighty-eight out of action, for no panzer cannon could make such a wreck.

"Sir," Miller called out. "The panzers are approaching."

Chalmers peered around the side of the Crusader's hull. The four panzers still mobile continued to move forward, their guns silent at last. Chalmers saw scars of bright metal and blackened steel plate here and there across the panzers' hulls, where numerous hits had failed to penetrate, most of them no doubt at long range.

The one mobile Panzer IV turned and began to come their way. Looking over at the lone crewman off to his right, Chalmers saw the man watch the panzer approach, then look in Chalmers' direction. Even at a distance, the look of resignation on the crewman's face was evident. Gathering himself up, the man stood, then raised his hands up high before stepping out from behind the burning tank.

The turret of the Panzer IV swung around in the man's direction, and Chalmers tensed, fearing the worst, but instead, the turret's hatch popped open, and the panzer commander appeared, an MP-40 in his hands. The German motioned with the barrel of his machine pistol, and the other man nodded, tentatively stepping further out.

Miller turned and looked at Chalmers. "Looks like the Jerries are willing to take prisoners, but I'll follow you, sir, whatever you decide."

Looking at their weapons, completely useless against the armoured behemoth in front of them, Chalmers knew there wasn't any point in throwing their lives away. By all accounts, both sides in this desert war had come to an unspoken agreement about treating prisoners fairly and decently. Thinking of Bob and Alfie, dead inside the tank he leaned against, or poor Wilson burned to ash and bone inside his own tank, Chalmers decided a German POW camp behind enemy lines was a far better fate than those recently suffered by his late comrades.

Chalmers muttered a curse, and set his Thompson on the ground. Miller saw this and nodded, doing the same with the Bren gun. The two men smiled at each other.

"Sorry old boy," Chalmers said. "Looks like we're in the bag."

The two men raised their hands and stepped out from behind the Crusader. The panzer commander turned and covered them with his machine pistol, a triumphant grin across his face.

"*Ja, Hände hoch*, Tommies! *Das ist gut!*"

FIFTEEN

The Airfield
November 17th, 0900 Hours

Everything hurt. His skull pounded, and dried blood covered one side of his head. His face felt as if it had been kicked in, and his lower lip was split and swollen. Every limb ached, with patches of skin scraped away along his shoulders, elbows, and knees. Both hands were sore and bloody, the side of his left hand bearing a large, nasty-looking cut along the edge of his palm. His back and ribs felt battered and bruised, and it hurt just to breathe. All in all, he was a broken, bloody mess.

But he was *alive.*

Harry Nelson opened his eyes and slowly raised himself up onto one elbow, wincing as raw skin grated against the desert sand. The sun was halfway overhead, and he raised his other arm to block out the light as he squinted and looked around him, assessing his situation.

Nelson lay among a dozen other men wearing British uniforms, most of them tankers. All of them looked to be in rough shape, displaying various states of injury, fatigue, and in more than a few cases, signs of near-escape from a fiery death. A few lay on the ground on top of a thin blanket, while others sat, staring around forlornly at each other. One man passed a metal bucket to another, who took a sip of water from a ladle, while another man nibbled with little enthusiasm on a hard biscuit. No one met his eye.

Three Germans stood guard around the prisoners, all of them with weapons at the ready. Two of the Germans carried MP-40s, while a third held a captured Thompson. Their guards all wore smug expressions on their faces - expressions Nelson wanted to violently erase with his knuckles. A thought occurred to him, and he ran his hands over himself, searching for his kit. His belt and webbing had been taken, along with all his other gear, but when he ran a hand across his chest, Nelson discovered the Germans hadn't found everything, and he forced himself to maintain a straight face.

Not so bloody clever, are you, Fritz?

"So, you didn't hit your head as hard as I thought."

Nelson turned around. Herring was sitting cross-legged behind him, a remnant of biscuit in his hand. The wiry little Commando had a bruised cheek and a cut over one eye, but other than that, he appeared in decent shape, although there was a considerable amount of dried blood all over the left side of his battledress.

"Don't know about that, I've got a bloody hard head," Nelson replied.

"No doubt," Herring said.

Nelson looked around again at the survivors. "Did that Kiwi of ours…?"

Herring shook his head and pointed at the blood all over his side. "Must have been hit by a shell from one of those armoured cars. He just about blew apart."

"Poor blighter," Nelson muttered. "Never knew what killed him, I wager."

Herring shrugged. "Better him than me. If he hadn't taken the hit, I would have."

"Right cold bastard, aren't you?" Nelson said, narrowing his eyes.

"Coming from you," Herring shot back, "that's a bloody compliment."

Nelson's hands balled into fists, and he moved to get up, but after a moment, common sense prevailed, and he relaxed with some effort. The situation was bad enough without fighting among themselves.

"I don't see any more of our lads," Nelson said after a moment, "from our squad or the other. Looks to be mostly the major's boys."

Herring nodded. "There's a fellow from the other recce element, one of the armoured car crewmen, but someone said they don't think he'll live through the day, even though the Germans patched him up. No other Commandos though. Not sure if that means the rest escaped, or they're dead."

"The last thing I remember is seeing our boys legging it away from the fight," Nelson said. "I hope they managed to get clear, but how the hell did we not get blown to bits?"

"They raked us with those cannons, and both left side wheels blew out. We started to fishtail and I heard you go over the side right before the engine took a couple of hits and died. I bailed out before I got perforated, and they chopped the truck up but good. The old girl caught fire and I had to give up the fight before she blew up next to me."

"Well, sod me for a game of soldiers, but this didn't turn out well," Nelson grumbled. He experimented with moving his arms, rolling his shoulders and wrists, and flexing at the elbow. Although everything hurt, he seemed to be without any serious injury.

Herring glanced around at the three guards, then leaned in close. "Did they find everything of yours?"

Nelson frowned. "What do you mean?"

"When they searched you, did they find everything? Do you have a bit of kit tucked away?"

Nelson looked towards the guards, but they seemed more intent on scanning the horizon than paying attention to their prisoners. Harry surreptitiously tapped his chest.

"Got me brass knuckles on a leather thong around me neck," he whispered.

Herring nodded and tapped a finger against his ankle. "They missed my switch-knife."

"Better than nothing, eh wot?" Nelson said with a sly grin.

"Nothing or no, we're still in the bag. And beyond our jailors, there's those monsters to contend with." Herring pointed to the other end of the airfield.

Nelson shielded his eyes and looked. There were four tanks leaguered at the southern end of the airfield. Three were Panzer IIIs, the last a larger IV. Another Panzer IV was slowly rumbling across the desert towards the others, escorted by one of the two light armoured cars. The remaining two armoured cars were off to the south-east, near the ravine where the other half of the recce element had gone - and probably been slaughtered. To the south and west, columns of smoke rose up from all along the horizon, showing where both friend and foe had met a fiery end.

Nelson turned back to Herring. "How many panzers do you suppose there were? I can't imagine just these few drubbed so many of our lads."

"I asked one of the tankers," Herring replied. "He said there were about a dozen, but that big gun firing from the airfield was an eighty-eight, and it knocked out a number of our tanks. Then there were the two Pak guns we didn't deal with."

"A right cock-up, it seems," Nelson said, gingerly running fingers along the wound in his scalp.

"So, what do we do?" Herring asked.

Nelson shook his head gingerly. "Nothing we bloody well can do right now. The other lads got away, and that great big show tomorrow might cause Jerry quite the fit. Who knows? Maybe by the end of the year, we'll be out of the bag, and it'll be us guarding a pack of Fritzes."

Herring scooted closer and leaned in. "Bollocks. I know you, Nelson. You're a braggart and a right tosser, but you're also a throat-cutter, a scoundrel, just like me. You're not going to sit on your great big arse and pick at fleas in some Jerry lock-up while the war goes on."

The two men locked eyes for a long moment, until finally, a smile curled Nelson's lips. "I knew there was something bloody wrong with you. Alright, you little wanker. We sit tight until tonight, feel out a few of these other lads, and then we make our move if the dice feel like they'll roll our way."

Herring nodded, then glanced past Nelson. "Jerries coming."

Nelson turned as a pair of German officers approached. One of them, a *Hauptmann* by his insignia, was dressed in the standard *DAK* uniform with a soft cap, while the other man, an *Oberleutnant*, wore a hard peaked cap with *Luftwaffe* insignia. The two men conversed in German for a few moments, before the senior officer addressed the British prisoners.

"Burial detail," the German said in unaccented English. "You will recover the bodies of your comrades, and then bury them. Our men will do the same with our dead. In a gesture of goodwill, we shall dig the graves together. You men fought hard this morning, and we respect that. The desert is no place to fight a war, if such a place does exist, and although you lost today, we have all suffered through these long months."

The German looked around the group sitting or lying before him, then pointed at one of the British. "You. You're an officer."

One of the tankers got to his feet with painful slowness. "Lieutenant Chalmers, E Squadron, 2nd Gloucestershire Hussars. Major Meade was killed in action this morning. I suppose that makes me the senior British officer present."

"Lieutenant Chalmers, do you guarantee the good behavior of these men?" the German asked.

Chalmers turned and eyed the men around him. "As long as we are treated well and fairly, there'll be no trouble. Now, sir, to whom have we surrendered ourselves?"

"I am *Hauptmann* Steiner, of the Regiment Brandenburg." the German replied. "This is *Oberleutnant* Hasek, of the *Luftwaffe*. I am now the senior officer here."

"Beg pardon, sir," Chalmers said. "What do you mean by 'now'?"

Steiner gave Chalmers a thin smile. "My commanding officer, *Major* Kessler, died during the battle as well. Now, come Lieutenant, let us bury him, along with whatever's left of your Major Meade."

Nelson, Herring, and the other British prisoners got to their feet, and covered by the gun muzzles of their German captors, walked out into the desert to go and bury their collective dead.

SIXTEEN

Twenty Miles South-West of the Airfield
November 17th, 1030 Hours

The four Chevrolet trucks - all that was left of Meadeforce - rolled to a stop a half-mile into the ravine. They'd spotted the broken ground after hours of driving through the desert, first due west, then turning to the south after consulting a map. A LRDG patrol some months ago had made a deep reconnaissance into Libya and noted some broken ground in the area, so Eldred and Price had decided to go there in order to hole up for the rest of the day and regroup.

Eldred dismounted from Lynch's truck, and the Irishman watched as the captain looked over his meagre command. They were only thirteen men - nine Commandos and four of the Desert Group. Barely a single squad's worth, and ill-equipped to fight any Germans they might encounter. Their sole heavy weapon was the 28mm "squeeze bore", the lightest of the German army's anti-tank guns. Aside from that, there were three Boys anti-tank rifles, seven machine guns, and their individual small arms.

"Alright lads, listen up," Eldred spoke, his voice carrying to every man. "We've suffered a terrible defeat at the hands of

149

the enemy this morning, and there's nothing we can do to change that. But we are alive, we are well-trained, and most of all, we want to go on to win the war. We will leaguer here for the rest of the day, so get some rest, tend to your kit, and make any necessary repairs. We will assess our supplies, ration accordingly, and in the morning we will make for friendly lines. Are there any questions?"

No one spoke up. Eldred looked each man in the eye. "Excellent. Corporal Bowen, I want you and your spotter on the top of this ravine. Make your way back to where we entered and set up an OP to make sure we haven't been followed. You men of the Desert Group, I want you to make a thorough examination of your trucks and the supplies of petrol, water, and food. The rest of you, inventory our weapons, ammunition, and any other ordnance. Sergeant McTeague?"

The Scottish sergeant nodded. "Aye, Captain?"

"That Boche anti-tank gun is your responsibility. Get it checked out, then make sure it is ready to be served and put to use."

"Yessir, right away. Higgins, you're with me."

"Corporal Lynch?" Eldred asked.

"Captain?" Lynch replied.

"I'm putting you in charge of the anti-tank rifles. Examine each in turn, make sure they are operational, and prepare them in case we are attacked."

"Good as done, sir," Lynch answered.

Moving aside a few parcels that had come loose during their flap across the desert, Lynch uncovered the Boys anti-tank rifle nestled along one side of the truck. He lifted the weapon by its carrying handle, grunting with the effort of moving the weapon's thirty-five pounds one-handed. Five feet long, and incredibly unwieldy, the bolt-action rifle fired a .55 calibre armour-piercing bullet. The blast and recoil of the weapon were astonishing, and despite being called an "anti-tank" rifle, it was all but useless against an actual tank. However, during their mission last month, a number of Boys rifle teams working together were able to cripple a couple of Autoblinda armoured cars at close range. Lynch thought the weapon's "success" during that encounter might be a case of damning with faint praise, but right now, it was the best they had next to their lone anti-tank gun.

Lynch opened a canvas satchel next to the rifle and pulled free one of the Boys' five-round magazines. He opened the rifle's bolt, checked its action to make sure the weapon was operating normally, and then seated the magazine. Satisfied that the rifle was battle-ready, Lynch slung his own personal weapon - his Thompson submachine gun - and moved to the next truck.

Lynch and the other men went about their tasks with a purpose, hoping to put from their minds thoughts of friends and comrades lost, the likelihood of their own capture or death at the hands of the Germans, and the difficult conditions all around them, which lessened their already slim chances of making it back to friendly lines. Lynch had to remind himself that, as bad as it was, he'd escaped from bad situations before. The battle for France in the summer of 1940 had been a nightmare; days upon days of retreating under constant attack from the Germans. Artillery barrages, Stuka dive-bomber attacks, and the ever-encroaching enemy infantry and panzer formations had driven them back without pause for weeks, and Lynch still vividly recalled standing in chest-deep water off the coast of Dunkirk, rifle laid across his shoulders to keep it out of the surf, waiting for the next boat to take him back to Blighty while geysers of water leapt into the air all around him from explosions and strafing runs.

So many men never made it off those bloody beaches, men like his squadmate Edwards, who'd reluctantly gone back with Lynch during the retreat from the battle at Arras to rescue their company commander, Captain Rourke, who'd been wounded by machine gun fire. Edwards and Lynch had retrieved Rourke and saved him from capture by the encroaching Germans, and for his actions, Lynch had been awarded the Military Medal upon returning to England. Rourke had lost his leg, but survived the evacuation, one of the last wounded men taken aboard ship before the decision was made to leave behind anyone who couldn't move unassisted. Poor Edwards, mentioned in dispatches for his part in the rescue, died on the Dunkirk beach, killed by a dive-bomber an hour before boarding a transport home.

It was during those last awful hours, cold and wet and under fire, helpless to do anything more than wait for rescue or death, that Lynch promised himself he'd get back into the fight as soon as possible. He'd felt such helpless rage, a dark, bloody rage as only an Irishman can conjure up within himself, and he knew it needed an outlet or it'd eat him up from the inside. When the opportunity presented itself to join Durnford-Slater's 3 Commando, Lynch unhesitatingly volunteered, and when Lord Pembroke made his offer to send Lynch over the Channel to assist the French partisans, Lynch had instantly accepted.

Lynch had believed at the time the Germans had a lot to answer for: Rourke's leg, Edwards' life, and all the other men in the Royal Irish Fusiliers he'd known and lost. Now, a year and a half later, that list was much longer, and much more personal.

153

An hour after the men had set about their tasks, everything seemed as ready as it would be, given their overall poor state. The Desert Group men reported that all four trucks were in good working condition, although two of the spare tyres had been shredded by enemy fire. Some of the petrol and drinking water had been lost for similar reasons, and one of the three Vickers guns had been disabled, its receiver dented beyond repair by a bullet. That left three Lewis light machine guns and two Vickers, along with the various rifles, SMGs, and sidearms of the men. In addition, they had a collective three dozen Mills Bombs and a handful of German stick-grenades.

The loss of petrol and water was troubling, especially given their distance from friendly resupply. The New Zealanders estimated they had just enough fuel to get back to Siwa, if the shortest route possible was taken. As for the water, every man was to be rationed four pints a day for all uses, down from the usual six. This was met with no small amount of grousing from the Commandos, who were still not as used to tight water rations as the LRDG men, but there was little choice in the matter. If they were careful, they'd have enough water to get them back to Siwa, with one full day's rations to spare, just in case.

By this time it was midday, and before lunch was prepared, the men took time to camouflage the trucks with the rolls of netting carried on each vehicle. Captain Eldred's greatest worry at the moment was being spotted by that Storch, so he sent Lance Corporal White and Corporal Lawless up onto the ridge with field glasses to stand watch for aircraft.

While dining on yet another meal of bully beef and biscuits - the latest in what now seemed an endless series of such meals - Lynch sought out Lieutenant Price.

"Savoring another one of our sumptuous feasts, Tommy?" Price asked.

"Oh, to be sure, just like Christmas dinner at the orphanage," Lynch replied.

Price gave a faint smile. "What's on your mind, Corporal?"

"I was wondering," Lynch began, "why we're spending an entire day tucked away in this ravine. Ought we to be escaping back into Egypt as soon as possible?"

Price took a moment to deliberately masticate an especially stubborn biscuit before answering. "The captain and I have discussed this at some length. He feels, and I am in agreement, that we're in significant danger of being found again by that recce plane if we try to arrow back across The Wire today. Come tomorrow, the offensive will begin, and all eyes will turn north, to where the fighting is taking place.

Once that happens, the last thing on Jerry's mind will be four trucks scarpering to the border."

Lynch thought for a moment about his officers' logic. At first blush, the decision didn't make sense; the longer they loitered behind enemy lines, the greater the risk of being rumbled. But the more he thought about it, the tactic reminded him of a crook who commits a robbery and runs a short distance, then finds a clever spot to hide and lay low while the bobbies run past, assuming the criminal is still on the run. Once the coast is clear, and the authorities have given up the chase, the crook emerges from hiding and escapes unnoticed. Lynch explained his line of thinking to Price, who chuckled good-naturedly.

"We didn't think of things in that light, but yes, that's just about spot-on," Price said. "Good to know there's a career for myself and the captain as scofflaws if we survive the war."

'If we survive the war', he says, Lynch thought to himself. *We'll be lucky to survive the next few days.*

As if to add insult to injury, he heard the droning of the Storch's engine, once again flying overhead.

SEVENTEEN

Outside the Airfield
November 17th, 1500 Hours

Steiner watched as one of the panzer crewmen shoveled spadefuls of sandy dirt onto the corpse of *Major* Kessler. The grizzled panzer commander had been struck in the side of the head by a bit of armour spalling and killed instantly. Steiner had examined the wound out of somewhat morbid curiosity; the thumb-sized hunk of metal had struck Kessler right behind the ear and buried itself deep inside the skull cavity. Steiner surmised that the terminal effect of the wound was probably little different than if Kessler had been shot in the side of the head with a pistol. More than likely, the *Major* never knew what killed him.

"Alive and fighting one instant, gone the next," Steiner said as he watched dirt cover Kessler's face. "When I go, that's how I want it to happen."

"Do you think the Tommies will be so accommodating, *Hauptmann*?" *Gefreiter* Werner asked, standing at Steiner's side.

"They are a painfully polite society," Steiner replied. "I imagine they would do their best to oblige, and probably ask the same in return."

Werner shook his head. "When I die, I want to know it is coming."

Steiner turned and looked at his companion. "That's morbid of you. Why would you say that?"

"Sir, when it is my time," Werner answered, "I want to know I am dying, but not without a fight. I want to look my killer in the eye and say 'This may be my death, but I am taking you with me.'"

Steiner pondered this for a moment with a smirk on his face. "That's a rather Teutonic way to end it. Positively Wagnerian. I think *der Führer* would approve."

Werner looked his superior in the eye for a moment, then curled his lip in disgust. He then turned and spat into the dust at his feet.

Steiner chuckled at Werner's reaction. He himself had no love for Adolf Hitler, and he wasn't a supporter of the Nazi party either, at least privately. Steiner knew Werner felt much the same way, as did a couple of the other surviving Brandenburgers. It was downright treasonous for a member of the *Heer*, never mind a soldier in an elite unit such as theirs, to publicly admit they did not subscribe to their ruler's ideologies. However, Steiner was a man with a talent for discerning other people's inclinations, and over the last two years, he'd come across a number of soldiers whose duty was directed towards the Fatherland, not *der Führer*.

The faint droning of an airplane's engine caught Steiner's attention, and he shielded his eyes with his hand and looked up. Coming from the south, he saw the flyspeck of a plane approaching.

"Does that sound like Hasek's Storch to you?" Steiner asked.

"Yes, sir. Should we prepare an anti-aircraft detail just in case?" Werner asked.

Steiner shook his head. "It's just one plane. If it's the British, they'll fly above our effective range anyway, so there's no point."

Taking his eyes from the sky, Steiner surveyed the grim task they'd been undertaking since that morning. The Germans, with fewer dead, were finishing their burial detail first. Looking back at Kessler, completely hidden under the dirt now, his panzer had been the only destroyed tank on the German side to not catch fire. A single armour-piercing round had penetrated the turret, spraying Kessler and his gunner, loader, and radio operator with lethal spalling. The driver had survived the hit and climbed past the carnage and out of the turret. The man had spent the rest of the battle slumped against the rear of the panzer, weeping in anger and frustration. It was Kessler's driver who worked the shovel to bury his commander now, fresh tears running down the man's face. Although Kessler's crew had only served together a few days, Steiner saw how deeply the older officer's death affected his driver.

Unfortunately for the rest of the burial detail, the other deaths hadn't been anywhere near as neat as Kessler's. Most of the dead panzer men had been badly burned, some beyond all recognition. It'd taken hours for most of the panzers to completely burn out, and in the worst cases, smoke and flames still flickered inside the scorched hulls. Steiner accepted that the crews of those wrecks would be little more than ash by the time their panzers were finished burning out.

The same was true for the British and their tank crews, of course. Steiner had checked on their progress several times during the day, and each time he'd witnessed some fresh horror. The Crusader tank, it seemed, caught fire rather easily, and the fires within them were especially fierce. He'd also been shocked at the devastating hits caused by the eighty-eight on such lightly-armoured tanks. In several cases, the armour-piercing shot had penetrated both sides of the hull, and there were no survivors from any of the tanks killed by that fearsome weapon. If the German high command were smart, they'd find a way to mount such a lethal instrument in a panzer chassis. The resulting vehicle would be immense, but the firepower it'd carry would be insurmountable.

The sound of an approaching automobile caused Steiner to turn around, and he saw Hasek approaching in his staff car. The plane had touched down mere moments ago, so Steiner presumed that whatever Hasek had seen, it was important.

"I've found them," Hasek said, as he pulled up next to Steiner and snapped the briefest of salutes.

"Found who?" Steiner asked.

"The remnant of the western flanking element, those desert trucks. I know where they went," Hasek explained.

Steiner nodded. He turned to Werner. "Keep an eye on things here, and when our men are finished, have them assist the British. Our boys won't like it, but I want these bodies in the ground before sundown."

"*Jawohl*," Werner said, and offered a salute.

Steiner returned the gesture, then hopped into Hasek's Kübelwagen. They were soon inside the airfield's command tent, and Hasek rolled out a large-scale map of the surrounding desert. Most of the terrain features had been hand-drawn by the aviator himself. After a few moments' work with a ruler and compass, Hasek tapped a finger against a penciled-in cut in the desert that appeared to be a ravine, several miles long.

"They disappeared into this," Hasek stated.

"You are sure?" Steiner asked. "It cannot be easy to spot four small vehicles from such a height."

Hasek gave him a triumphal smile. "It is them all right. I could not see their trucks inside the ravine, not with how the shadows were angled this afternoon, but I was able to follow their tracks."

"You were able to spot four sets of tyre tracks from a mile above the ground?" Steiner asked dubiously.

Hasek nodded. "One thread is hard to see at a distance, but many threads brought together make a rope. They weren't obeying proper spacing discipline, and kept too close together. The pattern was easy to see whenever they hit sandy ground, and in the afternoon light, tyre tracks are easier to see, as the shadows make them stand out. Once I knew what to look for, tracking them was child's play."

"And you're sure they're still in that ravine?" Steiner asked.

"I circled the area, and found no evidence of their departure. I think they've holed up there for the day. Perhaps they have wounded who need tending, or repairs need to be made to one of their trucks. It is a nice place to hide, and if they'd been more careful getting there, I wouldn't have seen them."

Steiner pondered the map for a moment. "What about the other element, the two who escaped from the ravine to the east?"

When the panzers had been found hiding in the low ravine by the British eastern recce element, their armoured cars and two of the lead trucks had been destroyed. However, the smoke and wreckage had prevented the panzers from engaging the last two vehicles. Steiner's men had made a sweep of a few kilometres around the airfield and had seen the tyre tracks leading out of the ravine and off into the east.

Hasek's lips drew into a thin line. "Unfortunately, I didn't find them. It may be the crew kept their heads better, and paid more attention to where they drove, staying to harder ground where tracks would be harder to spot from the air."

Steiner shook his head. "It is a small matter. We've got the armoured cars and the panzers, as well as the base defences. Half a dozen trucks scattered around the desert are no threat to us."

"So, what is our next move?" Hasek asked.

Steiner looked at his watch. "Two hours ago, I radioed in a report of the engagement to my superiors. They aren't particularly concerned with the activities of such a small enemy force, but they want us to remain vigilant."

"Makes sense," Hasek said. "As long as it isn't a large armoured assault, I can imagine they aren't too worried."

Steiner nodded. "However, I want to find out what the British were doing here. Once the burial detail is finished, I'm going to interrogate this Lieutenant Chalmers and learn what he knows."

Hasek raised an eyebrow. "Interrogate, you say?"

"Don't fret," Steiner chuckled. "Whatever the reason for this attack, I am certain they were not the lead element of some larger force, or we'd have seen them already, and you would have found some sign of their approach. No, I'm beginning to suspect this was something else, either a reconnaissance in force or some kind of diversion, and if that's the case, I want to know what purpose it served."

"And if he doesn't want to divulge the grand strategies of the British Eighth Army? Will one of your men beat it out of him?" Hasek asked.

Steiner tutted at the other officer. "Come now, *Oberleutnant*. Do you think me so cruel? Such barbarities are the tools of the simple-minded. I prefer a more nuanced approach."

Hasek shrugged. "I care not what you do to the Tommies. My brother died in a Bf-109 over the Channel last year. I have no pity for them."

"Well, you are welcome to sit in on the interrogation, but I doubt there will be any bloodshed," Steiner offered.

"I've got to oversee maintenance to my plane, but please let me know what you learn," Hasek replied. "I'll be with my mechanic if you need me."

The two men saluted each other and Hasek departed. Steiner stood for a minute, looking down at the map in front of him. A half-dozen recce trucks scattered about the desert were no threat to them - or were they? The truck they'd destroyed off to the west had a 20mm cannon mounted on it, dangerous to the armoured cars, but certainly not the much better-armoured Panzer IIIs and IVs. One of the trucks wrecked to the east had a 37mm anti-tank gun, and while that would be more dangerous, it wasn't a concern anymore. Steiner felt most of the heavy weapons carried by these Desert Group men were now out of the fight.

A shudder ran through Steiner as he recalled the ambush set for his armoured cars three weeks ago by men driving similar Chevrolet trucks. He remembered the gunner in his Autoblinda, killed in a gruesome manner by an anti-tank round punching through the turret next to him. Steiner bore a fresh scar on his leg from where a fragment of armour slashed him after another round crippled the car, forcing him and the two remaining crew members to bail out.

Steiner remembered glimpsing the portee-mounted anti-tank gun that fired on them, the truck it was mounted on exposing itself just enough to fire past the side of a low hill.

The weapon was identical to that mounted on the truck they'd destroyed this morning. And as he thought about it, he realized the destroyed 20mm autocannon he'd seen was the same model of Italian weapon his *Bersaglieri* had fielded.

In his mind's eye, Steiner recalled the group of British prisoners he'd addressed that morning, and while most of the tank crewmen had sat there, slumped and dejected, with only Chalmers standing up and speaking for them, two men off to one side had stared at him, silent and unbowed. Steiner remembered one of the men, the larger of the two, had sat with his left arm towards Steiner, and the patch on his arm differed from that worn by the tankers.

Steiner spun around and exited the tent. Outside, one of his Brandenburgers stood watch, a machine pistol across his chest.

The sentry saluted Steiner. "*Hauptmann?*"

"Go to the British burial detail," Steiner ordered. "There are two prisoners I need brought to me. Each wears this badge on his uniform."

Kneeling, Steiner unsheathed his combat knife and drew a crude sketch of the Commando patch in the sand.

EIGHTEEN

The Airfield
November 17th, 1530 Hours

Nelson knew nothing good could come from being escorted back to the airfield for "questioning" by the German commanding officer. He and Herring walked several paces in front of their guard, and although the two Commandos had shared a sidelong glance at each other, they both knew now was not the time to try and make a move.

Inside the command tent, the two Commandos were directed to sit in folding wooden camp chairs. Along with the soldier who'd escorted them, another soldier stood next to the German officer, cradling an MP-40. All three Germans bore completely neutral expressions. Once seated, Nelson and Herring were offered tin cups of water, and allowed to gather their thoughts for a moment.

Finally, the German officer spoke.

"I do not recall seeing either of you two gentlemen during the attack on the *Bersaglieri* outpost to the south of us, almost three weeks ago. However, there is no doubt now in my mind that you participated in that action. The autocannon mounted to your truck, it is a Breda, a Model 35, and we had two just like it for anti-aircraft defence. The night of the attack, a squad of Commandos infiltrated the base, and they captured one of our Bredas, and turned it on the *Bersaglieri*. I saw what it did from the top of the fortress wall, and I do not lie when I say it turned my guts to water. I had never seen men reduced to such horrid things in that manner before."

The German paused, as if waiting for Nelson or Herring to say something, but both men remained silent. After a moment, he began to speak again.

"Although it wounds my professional pride to say this, I admire you men for defeating me and the men under my command that night. It was a very brave thing, sneaking through the dark such a distance, scaling the ridge, silencing the Italian sentries. That takes boldness, and discipline. Were you men Germans, I would be proud to serve with you."

Again the German paused, and both Nelson and Herring remained silent. Nelson wasn't sure where the German was going with his monologue, but he was worried it was going to end with a machine pistol being put to use.

"Unfortunately," the German continued, "You are the enemy. You bested me once, but now the fortunes of war have turned against you. Your strike force is destroyed, its men killed, captured, or scattered. Whatever your intended mission was, you have failed to accomplish it."

Unable to bear the German's ramblings any longer, Nelson cleared his throat.

"Sorry mate," he said, "but is there a bloody point to this speech?"

The German's face froze for a moment, before he let out a laugh and slapped his knee. "Excellent! You have great spirit. I admire that. Here you are, captured and many kilometres from nowhere, guns pointed at you, and the first words out of your mouth are insults."

Nelson shrugged. "Not much of an insult, really. If that's what you're looking for, I could have a few choice words about your mum's fanny."

The German officer gave Nelson a smirk, but the guard next to him snarled and stepped forward, slapping Nelson across the face with a vicious backhand. Nelson's head snapped back, and a thin line of blood trickled from his split lip.

Recovering from the blow, Nelson grinned. "Speaking of mums, mine hit me harder'n that when I stole nips from her gin bottle."

Nelson's assailant drew back his hand as if to strike again, but the officer waved him back. After a moment of glaring at his subordinate, the officer turned to Nelson.

"I apologize for that. I do not condone beating an unarmed man, a prisoner in my care, and certainly not for anything other than a harmless comment."

Nelson shrugged. "Well, Fritz, ain't you a gentleman. Blast us all to bits this morning, and now you beg pardon for a lady's tickle on me chin."

The officer shook his head. "Killing is the unfortunate business of war, but that doesn't mean its savagery is unlimited. I have won this day, but many of our comrades are dead. Although it pleases me to have defeated you, I wish there hadn't been such loss of life on both sides of the battlefield."

"Well bless me heart," Nelson muttered. "A bloody Nazi with a conscience."

The officer's lips drew together in a thin line, and for a moment, Nelson wondered if he'd said one word too many. But after a moment, the officer glanced at the guard who'd brought them in, and then composed himself.

"Six of your reconnaissance trucks escaped this morning," he said. "Four fled to the west, and two escaped to the east. While we haven't yet found the two trucks to the east, we do know where the others are hiding. I believe those are the men you tried to save with your actions this morning?"

Nelson said nothing, although he felt the blood drain from his features. The officer smiled.

"A squadron of fast tanks, plus armoured cars and mechanized scouts, destroys an Italian supply depot in the southern desert. The next day, they try to destroy this airfield, despite losing all their supply vehicles. What I want to know is, why?"

Nelson didn't say anything, although he noticed Herring shift slightly next to him.

"Sorry, guv. Can't help you there," Nelson answered. "Us, we's just a couple of dumb riflemen, eh? We leave the decisions up to the quality, the officers. Off to fight and die for King and Country, that's us!"

The German gestured to the stripes on Nelson's sleeve. "You're a corporal. That's not very far up the chain of command, but I know how non-commissioned officers are - you've got your own ways of finding out what's going on, even when you're supposed to be kept in the dark. I cannot imagine you don't have at least a theory as to the nature of your mission."

"It's like the corporal says," Herring spoke up. "We go where we're told, like a couple of good soldiers, eh? The less we know, the less we can tell the likes of you if we wind up in the bag. Looks like that was a smart decision."

The officer scratched his chin for a moment. "I am not sure I buy these pleas of ignorance. So, I will offer you a little incentive." He clasped his hands behind his back and began to pace in front of Nelson and Herring. "We know where to find the men who escaped to the west. There can only be a handful, perhaps a dozen, certainly no threat to us now. However, until I know the nature of your assignment, I cannot be sure. If you can convince me those men pose no threat, that you are not the advance element of some larger force, I will be content to leave those men to their fate, out in the desert. Doubtless they are resourceful enough to make their way back to Egypt.

"On the other hand, if you refuse to cooperate, I will have no choice but to hunt them down, and either capture or kill them, in order to maintain the security of this installation. I have three armoured cars and five panzers at my disposal. I don't believe it will end well for your Commando brethren, no matter how brave or skillful they are. Now, what is your decision? Are you still going to maintain this fiction of ignorance?"

Nelson and Herring turned and looked at each other for a long moment. Nelson knew his own opinion on the matter, but the wiry rifleman was always difficult to read, and the rumor amongst the men was that Herring was some kind of knife-man before the war, an underworld murderer for hire. Nelson had always taken such rumors with a grain of salt, but you never knew another man's mettle until it was bent to the breaking point.

"Well?" Nelson asked Herring. "What'll it be, mate?"

Herring turned to the German. "How's about you get stuffed, you poncy git?"

For the second time that evening, the officer stood goggle-eyed, shocked by Herring's answer, before he threw his head back and laughed out loud.

"You English never disappoint me!" he said. "If you were Italians or Frenchmen, I think you might have told me what you knew, or at least, made up some fiction to dangle before me as bait. But no, you throw insults instead."

"See?" Nelson said with a smile. "We've got our reputation to uphold. Matter of honor and all that."

The German just shook his head. "I hope your little jest is worth the lives of your countrymen." He walked to the tent flap and pulled it aside, gesturing towards the leaguered panzers and armoured cars. "I'm going to take my three scout cars and one of those great big Panzer IVs with me this afternoon. We're going to go and find your friends, and I'm going to shell them to bits with that seventy-five millimetre howitzer. I'll regret killing them, for I am sure they are all good men. But I cannot leave them free to travel about the desert when I don't know the purpose behind your mission."

The officer turned to the two guards and said something in their native tongue. The two men saluted, and one moved to exit the tent, while the other watched Nelson and Herring,

173

clearly tasked with keeping an eye on the two prisoners. The officer stepped halfway out of the tent, then turned back to look at his captives one last time.

"The blood of those men will be on your hands, gentlemen. Not mine. *Auf wiedersehen*."

With that, the officer and one of his men departed the tent. The lone guard left behind shifted his feet and covered Nelson and Herring with the muzzle of his machine pistol. A moment later, the second soldier returned with two lengths of rope, and he bound Nelson and Herring to their chairs while the other man covered them.

Having secured their prisoners, the two soldiers gave their captives one last look before stepping outside the tent. A moment later, the smell of cigarette smoke wafted through the tent flap.

"I could bloody well use a fag right now," Nelson grumbled.

Herring leaned as close to Nelson as he could without falling over. "Watch what you say," he whispered. "The taller Jerry speaks English."

Nelson thought for a moment. "Right, that's good to remember. Now, can you get to your sticker?"

"No. We'll have to figure that out when the time is right," Herring whispered.

Nelson looked around the tent. There wasn't anything except for them and their chairs. "We bloody well better. Can't let that smug Jerry wanker get to Tommy and Rhys and the other lads."

Herring looked Nelson in the eye. "When night comes, we'll make our move."

"You're a right scary bastard, you know that?" Nelson asked.

"That's what your mum says when I pay her a visit," Herring whispered with a grin.

Nelson scowled. "Tosser."

After a moment's silence, the two men shifted in their wooden camp chairs, trying to find a comfortable position, and began their wait until dark, while outside, the sound of engines starting carried to them from the panzer leaguer.

NINETEEN

Thirty Kilometres South-West of the Airfield
November 17th, 1800 Hours

Steiner peered through his field glasses at the terrain before him. A kilometre away, the desert floor gently rose about twenty metres before levelling out again. From this distance, a thin crack in the rise was visible, probably only a handful of metres wide, but Steiner knew it was his quarry's hiding place. The tyre tracks - visible all around them - pointed right at the split, and it was the perfect place to hide from aerial observation.

It was also a dangerous place to try and take by force. A small contingent of stout-hearted defenders could choke such a narrow passage with their attackers' bodies, all the while falling back whenever pressed too hard. Although he had the clear advantage in firepower, Steiner didn't want to underestimate his enemy again. Furthermore, while he had all three armoured cars and the Panzer IV with him, he'd only been able to justify "borrowing" Hasek's ten-man security force. Even though he had seniority over Hasek, Steiner was still the outsider, and there was no quicker way to earn the enmity of those under your command than usurping their authority with no greater justification than that authority alone.

Steiner lowered his field glasses and looked around him. To his left, the Panzer IV's commander, a *Feldwebel* named Mueller, looked at him. Mueller's tank had been immobilized with a shredded track near the end of the battle that morning, and although Steiner had been reluctant to trust the repair job and take Mueller's panzer with him, its commander had insisted. Mueller's pride had suffered more than his panzer, and Steiner knew the man wanted to take it out on any British left ready to offer up a fight.

"Well, *Hauptmann*? What are your orders?" Mueller asked.

Steiner climbed out of the SdKfz 232's turret hatch and made his way down over the car's hull. He gestured for Mueller to wait, then walked back to the six-wheeled Krupp-Protze cargo truck at the back of their column. The infantry squad's leader, an old veteran named Huber, stood up and saluted.

"*Hauptmann*, your orders?" Huber asked.

"I want you to take your squad and advance to the cleft in the rise. Confirm that the tracks lead directly into the cleft, and look for signs of defence. Then, split your squad into two elements and move up the rise, then patrol along the top of the ravine."

Huber nodded. "What kind of resistance do you expect we're facing?"

"There should only be about a dozen men," Steiner answered. "But those desert reconnaissance trucks were well-armed with machine guns. Be careful and look for strong points that might conceal dismounted MGs. I'll send one of the cars with you, and the rest of us will follow a few hundred metres back."

Huber saluted and spoke to the driver. A few seconds later, the Krupp-Protze began to move towards the rise. Steiner gestured towards the commander of the first SdKfz 222, indicating that he should move forward with the infantry. The commander, one of his Brandenburgers, nodded and shouted an order down into the crew compartment before charging his 20mm autocannon.

Steiner climbed back into his own armoured car and watched the two vehicles depart. "Driver, follow two hundred metres back," he ordered.

The five vehicles moved across the desert at a cautious pace. Steiner wasn't especially worried, but they were terribly exposed out here, and until he'd dealt with these Commandos, he was going to be on edge. Glancing to the west, Steiner realized the cover of night was fast approaching. He didn't fancy navigating a narrow ravine in the dark and under fire.

The two lead vehicles were a half-kilometre from the cleft when Steiner heard the distant crack of a high-powered rifle. Raising his field glasses, he scanned the terrain ahead of him and saw nothing, but there was another shot, this one from a heavier-calibre weapon. He turned and focused on the truck carrying the infantry squad, and saw the ten men bailing out the back of the Krupp-Protze, the truck unmoving. A second later, the deep, slow *thumpthumpthump* of the lead armoured car's autocannon reached his ears, and Steiner saw the cloud of dust rising into the air in front of the car as the weapon's immense blast stirred the sand around it.

There was a *pang* of metal striking metal to his left, and Steiner looked down to see a bright streak of smeared copper and lead on the top of the turret by his elbow.

Sniper!

Dropping into the turret, Steiner closed the hatch just as a second round ricocheted away inches from his hand. Werner, serving as his gunner, looked up at Steiner in surprise.

"Someone is shooting at us!" Werner exclaimed.

"Obviously, you *Dummkopf*. Now lay down some covering fire!"

"Where? I have no target!" Werner asked.

"He's got to be somewhere along the ridge," Steiner snarled. "Get on the MG and lay a belt's worth down along the right-hand side!"

Steiner keyed his radio mic. "All units. Lay down covering fire. Car Three, suppress the left-hand ridgeline. Mueller, bracket the cleft with high-explosive."

For the next few seconds, the air was filled with the sounds of cannons and machine guns. Steiner peered through the vision blocks and observed the detonations of autocannon and howitzer shells.

He picked up his microphone again. "Mueller, move up and provide shelter to Huber's squad. The truck must be immobilized, so we'll have to pull them back out of range."

A much heavier impact rang through the hull, and Steiner looked over to see a noticeable dent about the size of his thumb in the armour plate. He placed his hand gently on the bulge, feeling the heat of the distressed metal.

"Anti-tank gun?" Werner asked.

Steiner shook his head. "At this range, even a light gun would penetrate us. That was one of their heavy rifles, the ones they used on our Italian cars. We're out of their effective range, but they can still tear up the transport, and rip a man in half."

Peering through the vision blocks, Steiner watched the Panzer IV roll up alongside the Krupp-Protze. As soon as the

180

panzer stopped, the ten infantrymen scuttled from behind their transport and clustered behind the larger armoured vehicle. Using his field glasses, Steiner watched as the panzer began to reverse slowly, the infantry staying a pace or two ahead of its progress, heads down and shoulders hunched, hoping to avoid drawing attention from the British sniper. All the while, the three armoured cars fired short bursts of machine gun and cannon fire, trying to suppress the hidden shooters.

"We'll pull back to fifteen hundred metres away from the rise," Steiner ordered over the wireless. "Cease fire, we're just wasting ammunition."

Minutes later, Steiner crawled out of his car's side hatch. He'd arranged the panzer and his much larger armoured car so they presented their flank to the rise, offering maximum protection to anyone disembarked. The infantry were kneeling next to the panzer, the men having a smoke and looking disgruntled.

"What happened?" Steiner asked Huber.

The infantry sergeant made a sour face. "The sniper took out the driver, killed him instantly. Then the engine block took several hits from something much heavier."

"One of their anti-tank rifles," Steiner said.

"The transport is dead, whatever they hit it with," Huber replied. "I saw oil puddling underneath the engine while we were in cover."

"*Scheisse*," Steiner muttered, then looked to the horizon. The sun would be down within the hour, not enough time to deal with the situation.

"Since the day is almost over, we'll bivouac here for the night," Steiner told the men around him. "Well before dawn, Huber's squad will move ahead and close the distance, swinging wide in a flanking manoeuvre before slipping up that rise. When the sun comes up, we'll use the panzer's howitzer and the car's MGs to keep their heads down. They'll be so busy avoiding that incoming fire, Huber and his men will be able to get close and eliminate the snipers before they can recover. Once the top of the rise is cleared, we'll move the panzer into the ravine and shell anything that moves, while the infantry provide cover from up above, and the cars circle around and press on to cut off any chance of escape."

The men around him nodded, and with that, Steiner dismissed the men to go about setting up camp for the night. He caught Huber's attention.

"I know these bastards," Steiner said in a low voice. "Make sure the sentries work in teams, keep them close, and above all, remain vigilant. These men, they aren't afraid of the dark."

182

TWENTY

The Airfield
November 18th, 0100 Hours

After being fed an evening meal and taken to the latrine, Nelson and Herring were placed back inside their tent by two guards. This time, instead of sitting on chairs, they were tied back-to-back, bound to the wooden support pole in the center of the tent. It was certainly more comfortable than trying to sleep in a hard wooden camp chair all night, but it also meant Herring's switch-knife, their only hope of escape, was further out of Nelson's reach.

The two men agreed to sleep in shifts, and after the guards changed late into the night, Nelson waited a full hour before gently nudging Herring awake with his shoulder.

"It's time, mate," Nelson whispered.

"I need to get higher in order to bend my leg around, so I can move my foot close enough for you to reach," Herring replied.

"Brace yourself against the tent pole, and I'll do the same. Then we'll push with our legs and raise ourselves up," Nelson explained.

"You're twice my size, you'll topple the bloody tent!"

"Guess you'll just have to put your sodding back into it, eh wot? C'mon now, on the count of three."

Seconds later, the two men strained, and slowly - painfully slowly - they began to inch their way up the tent pole. Their wrists soon began to bleed from the rough fibres of their bindings digging in, and their hands grew slippery with blood as they tried to maintain a grip on the wooden pole. Despite the cold of the desert night, sweat poured down their faces and their arms, chilling the men as it dried, while making their grip that much more precarious. Their heels dug furrows in the sandy floor, as each man fought against gravity and their awkward position. Several times, the tent pole swayed dangerously, and the men froze as the tent fabric pulled taut and tugged against the other poles and stays. If the Germans outside the tent saw it move, they'd come in and investigate, and the jig would be up.

After what seemed like an eternity, the two men reached a crouching position, and with a grunt of pain, Herring managed to bend and twist his leg behind him. Slowly, the two men lowered themselves back down, until Herring was kneeling and Nelson was seated behind him. Herring pushed his foot back and towards Nelson's hands.

"Up to you now," Herring whispered. "Try not to bloody hamstring me with my own blade."

Nelson's fingers crawled up Herring's calf, until they reached the top of his high woolen sock. He pulled the material down with frustrating slowness, his hand cramping from the awkward angle, fingers sticky with drying blood. Cursing at his bindings, Nelson grimaced against the pain as he rotated his wrist back and forth hard against the rope, causing more blood to flow and providing just enough lubrication to add the necessary freedom to his movements.

At last, Nelson's fingers made contact with the smooth metal of the switch-knife. Carefully, he pulled the knife free from the soft chamois leather of Herring's ankle sheath. Turning the knife in his hands, Nelson pointed the weapon in what he hoped was the right direction and engaged the spring release. The knife snapped open with a faint *click*, and Herring jerked against his bindings.

"You clumsy berk, you got my leg!" Herring whispered.

"Shut your gob and let me work here," Nelson shot back.

It took another ten minutes for Nelson to angle the knife just right, and slowly, clumsily, saw through the bindings around Herring's wrists. More than once he slipped and jabbed or nicked Herring's forearms, but the two men remained silent. Finally, the last of the rope fibres parted, and Herring's hands were free. After a few more minutes of work, he escaped from the other bindings holding him to the tent pole, and with a soft grunt of pain, Herring eased himself out

185

of the awkward position and stood up straight at last, massaging circulation back into his limbs and examining the cuts and abrasions along his arms.

"Last time I count on you to do any clever work with a knife. Carved me up like a Christmas ham," Herring muttered.

"Don't just bloody stand there whining about a few scratches," Nelson growled. "Cut me loose!"

Herring bent down and took his knife from Nelson's bloody hand, and after scrubbing the weapon clean with a handful of sand, he sliced through his squadmate's bindings with a few deft moves. Nelson rolled onto his side and stood, cursing softly and rubbing his backside.

"Me bum's asleep," he whispered.

"Now who's whining?" Herring replied.

The two men spent a couple of minutes just stretching and limbering up their bodies, with eyes always glued to the tent flaps leading outside. Once they were sufficiently ready, Nelson reached inside his undershirt and pulled out a leather thong. At the end, a pair of vicious-looking brass knuckles dangled. Nelson snapped the leather with a sharp tug, then slipped the weapons over his fingers, his hands forming fists as he tested the fit. When he was satisfied, Nelson nodded.

Working silently, Herring dropped down to the ground and crawled to the edge of the tent. He lifted the bottom edge of the tent fabric and peered out for a few seconds, then shifted to another position, eventually making his way all around the perimeter of the tent. Finally, he stood up and approached Nelson, bringing his mouth close to Nelson's ear as he whispered.

"There's two guards right outside the tent. I don't see any lights or movement, but there's just enough moonlight to tell we're at one end of the installation, furthest from the Jerry armour. We're maybe a hundred yards from the other prisoners, but I can't be sure from here."

Nelson nodded. "We deal with these two bastards, then make our way along the backside of the tents, near the outer perimeter. Kill any sentries we think we can take quiet-like, hiding otherwise. Once we get close to where the other lads are kept, we hit their guards like a bloody hammer and get guns in the hands of as many men as we can. Then, we fight hard and make for those bloody panzers. If we get a few of our tankers inside one, Jerry'll piss his britches."

At that, the two Commandos slipped close to the tent flaps, and using his knife, Herring cut the ties securing them together. With infinite care, he parted the flaps, revealing the two guards standing only a pace from the opening on either side. Both Germans were wearing their soft caps, but were otherwise fully armed and equipped.

Before the guards took notice of the disturbance behind them, the two Commandos struck. Nelson came up behind his target and wrapped his forearm around the guard's throat. Before the man could react, Nelson hammered his fist into the guard's kidney, the brass knuckles magnifying the force of the blow. The guard's back arched and he gurgled, unable to scream with Nelson's arm clamped around his throat like a vice. Nelson punched again and again, until his victim's legs went out from underneath him. With a savage jerk, Nelson twisted the guard's neck until there was a hideous crunching noise, and the guard's body spasmed and flopped for a moment before shuddering and going still. Nelson dragged the corpse back inside the tent, and as he did so, he saw Herring tear his knife free of the other guard's neck, an arc of spurting blood gleaming in the moonlight. As the second guard sagged to the ground, Herring dragged him inside the tent by his webbing.

The two men said nothing as they stripped the guards' bodies of anything useful. Nelson's victim carried an MP-40 and a pair of three-magazine ammunition pouches, as well as a fighting knife, an electric torch, and a stick grenade. Herring's victim had a Kar98K rifle, pouches for stripper clip-fed ammunition, and a bayonet. Herring eyed Nelson's machine pistol enviously, but Nelson shook his head.

"Not a bloody chance, mate. Now, let's get moving."

The two men finished buckling on the German webbing, and they both pulled on the service caps each man had worn in order to better disguise their silhouettes in the dark. Then, they slipped out of the tent and snuck around behind it, careful to avoid the ropes and stakes holding the tent up. Scanning the area around them, Nelson gave the signal to advance, and they began to move behind the various tents and other structures that made up the airfield installation. As they passed the Storch observation plane and its refueling lorry Nelson sighed, wishing he had an explosive more sophisticated than a single hand grenade.

Once beyond the Storch, they approached the wireless tent and its wooden antenna tower. Ahead of them, both Commandos saw the glow of a cigarette indicating the presence of a sentry standing in the lee of the tent, enjoying a late-night smoke. Herring looked to Nelson, who nodded and reached for Herring's rifle. Unburdened of his long gun, Herring dropped to the ground, and over the next couple of minutes, slithered like a snake towards his quarry.

The only sign of Herring's attack was the cigarette's glowing tip as it flew from the sentry's mouth and arced through the air, bouncing on the ground in a brief shower of sparks. Nelson counted to ten before moving forward in a crouch, until he saw the dark outline of Herring kneeling over the dead sentry. Herring slung the sentry's rifle and ammunition pouches, tucking a stick grenade into his belt, before taking the other rifle from Nelson. For a moment, the moonlight crossed Herring's features, and Nelson saw the man was smiling, the expression one wears after hearing a good joke. Herring saw Nelson looking at him and his smile grew even wider.

"Like putting a baby down for his nap," Herring whispered. "Didn't even know what happened until it was all over."

"You're a nutter, that's what you are," Nelson replied. "C'mon now, let's move."

The two men continued on, slipping around and behind several more tents. Now and then a sentry was seen at a distance, but they didn't encounter another in their way. Nelson sensed this was a disappointment to Herring, who tensed with excitement every time a sentry appeared, looking to Nelson as would a hunting dog, begging to be let off the leash.

Eventually they approached a more open area, where the moonlight illuminated still forms lying on the ground, surrounded by a crude rope fence and guarded by a trio of sentries. Nelson gestured to two guards who were nearest them and pointed to his chest, then pointed to Herring and the last guard, in turn. Herring nodded, then brought up his rifle. Nelson unfolded the wire stock of the MP-40 and tucked

190

it into his shoulder, settling the weapon's sights on the right-most sentry. To preserve his night vision as much as possible, Nelson closed his off-hand eye.

"*Now*," he whispered.

With a soft squeeze of the trigger, Nelson fired three rounds from the MP-40, the 9mm slugs stitching the guard from belly to shoulder. The guard dropped, and before he hit the ground, Nelson was firing on his second target. A longer four-round burst spun the man around and sent him tumbling into the sand, tangled in his rifle sling. Herring's shot, a moment after Nelson's, caught the third guard high in the chest and kicked him right off his feet.

The two Commandos broke into a low sprint and covered the short distance to the prisoners' pen. Men were cursing and sitting up or crouching, bewildered faces staring around wide-eyed, looking for a threat. Nelson scooped up a rifle from the closest corpse and tossed it to a tank crewman, who managed to catch it before taking the rifle's bolt in his face.

"What the blazes?" the man cried out.

"Jailbreak, lads!" Nelson answered. "Grab their weapons and make for those bloody panzers!"

With that, Nelson spun around and pulled the stick grenade from his belt. Twisting away the cap, he tugged on the arming loop and threw the grenade as hard as he could towards the wireless tent. The grenade sailed through the air and tumbled into the tent, detonating with a loud *crack* and a flash of high explosive. A scream came from inside the tent, slowly trailing off into a whimper.

All around him, the tankers were coming to their senses. Three other men were armed in short order from the bodies around them and the spare rifle Herring carried, and not a moment too soon, as the first Germans arrived and began firing. Immediately, one of the tank crewmen went down, a rifle bullet blowing away part of the man's face, before Nelson turned and cut down the German responsible with a burst of slugs.

"Move it!" he shouted. "We've got to take their armour!"

The men surged forward, only to drop and cower in the sand as a hail of machine pistol slugs whipped through the air all around them. Nelson, Herring, and a couple of the tankers returned fire, but the speed with which the Germans were responding made headway impossible.

"It's the crewmen!" Lieutenant Chalmers shouted at Nelson. "They bivouacked with their panzers!"

As if on cue, the growl of an engine coming to life reached them from the far side of the airfield.

Nelson turned to Chalmers. "The cannons on those tanks, do they fire high explosive?"

Chalmers nodded. "The big one, the Panzer IV, has a howitzer, and the others can all fire HE, but they don't need to, and they won't in such close quarters. They'll just use the machine guns, and that'll be enough, because we don't have anything that can stop them."

Nelson pointed back towards the tents. "Sir, get your men in amongst the tents and clear out any Germans left there. The panzers won't fire on the tents for fear of hitting their own. Herring will stick with you, he's a right terror when Jerries are around."

Chalmers nodded. "What about you?"

"I'm going to get me hands on a bigger gun," Nelson said, ducking as a burst of machine gun fire snapped overhead. "And, to use it, I need your best gunner."

Chalmers looked around for a moment, then grabbed a man by the arm and swung him around. "Miller, you're going with the corporal. Do whatever he tells you."

Miller nodded, looking a bit at sea, but he saluted nonetheless. "Yes, sir!"

Nelson turned to leave, but Chalmers caught his sleeve. "Corporal, exactly where are you going?"

"I'm going to commandeer that ruddy great big cannon of theirs," Nelson shouted. "The eighty-eight."

TWENTY-ONE

The Airfield
November 18th, 0215 Hours

Nelson snapped on the electric torch, and the beam illuminated the inside of the tent. Towering above them, the gun shield of the eighty-eight showed signs of recent battle damage; dents and pits in the steel marked where machine gun slugs had bounced off, and there was a fist-sized hole in the upper right-hand corner where a tank's armour-piercing shell had struck.

"Bloody hell," Miller whispered. "Now, this is a cannon! It's a sodding monster!"

"Can you operate it?" Nelson asked.

Miller stepped around the gun shield and Nelson followed, the torch lighting their way. Several opened ammunition crates were scattered around the gun, and a dozen or so spent shell casings littered the ground between the rear of the gun carriage and the back end of a large German half-track. Miller walked up to the weapon's controls, his gaze tracking over the wheels and levers, the gears and pistons that made up the great cannon. He ran his hands over the breech, as if tracing the weapon's method of operation in his mind.

"Aye, I can handle this. Semi-automatic sliding breech block, mechanisms for traverse, elevation, and firing. I'll need you to load it and trip the firing lever, and it'd be nice to have a third man to feed you the shells, but two men can do this in a pinch."

Nelson nodded. "Alright, let's get at it."

"We're going to need more visibility," Miller said. "I've got to see the targets better, and we need a wider field of view."

"What we need is a Very pistol," Nelson muttered. He dug around in the back of the half-track parked behind the eighty-eight. There were unopened crates of shells, as well as entrenching tools, lengths of chain, cleaning instruments for the gun, and other miscellanea. Finally, he found a small metal case that looked about the right size. Opening it, Nelson found a flare gun and a number of flare cartridges.

"Bloody brilliant," he muttered.

"I need my field of view!" Miller repeated.

"Right." Nelson moved back to the front of the gun and drew out the fighting knife he'd taken from the sentry. Working fast, he cut away the tent flaps and the side of the tent in the direction of where the German armour had been leaguered.

"Good," Miller said. "Now I can traverse the gun so it's aiming down the runway."

"The runway?" Nelson asked.

"If it was us, we'd move up the runway in column, bringing our turret MGs to bear on targets as we passed. Nice clear path, don't have to worry about obstacles or running over one of our mates stepping out from behind a tent."

Nelson nodded and stepped away from the gun as Miller rapidly spun the traversing wheel, the massive gun barrel slowly turning to the left until it was pointed down the entire length of the airfield. Off in the distance, they heard the sounds of engines roaring and the squealing of tank treads, the chatter of machine guns and the crack of rifles. In the dim moonlight, the looming shapes of panzers were just visible turning onto the far end of the runway.

"We need those Very lights," Miller said.

"Once we fire, they'll be gunning for us," Nelson warned. "How fast can you kill four tanks?"

"With this?" Miller asked. "As fast as you can load fresh rounds and pull the lever. Now, grab a shell and load."

Nelson reached into a half-emptied crate and pulled out a heavy armour-piercing shell. With Miller's direction, he slammed it home into the open breech, noticing how the breech locked closed once the shell was inserted.

"Now, send up the flare," Miller said.

Nelson snapped a fat cartridge into the flare pistol, then stepped to the edge of the tent. Aiming the pistol into the air, he pulled the trigger, and with a *pop*, the flare fizzled up into the sky for several seconds, before bursting into bright light several hundred yards in the air.

"Get behind the gun shield and fire!" Miller shouted.

Nelson jumped back and ducked behind the shield, then grabbed the firing lever and gave it a hard tug. The blast from the gun was enormous, like being struck by a sodden pillow in the face, and Nelson jumped as the gun recoiled back violently next to him. The breech snapped open at the end of its journey and kicked the spent shell free in a puff of burnt propellant smoke before the recoil mechanism returned it to its firing position.

"Missed! Loader, reload!" Miller ordered.

Nelson grabbed another shell and slammed it home in the still-smoking breech. Miller fiddled with the guns aiming mechanisms for a moment.

"Now, fire!"

This time, Nelson leaned far to the left and peered out around the edge at the oncoming panzers as he fired the gun. The first tank, one of the smaller Panzer IIIs, was perhaps two hundred yards away when the eighty-eight's shell struck. The armour-piercing round impacted at the top of the tank's gun mantlet, just to the left of the gun. There was a huge flash of sparks and white-hot metal fragments spinning through the air, and Nelson saw the top of the turret ripped open, flames licking upwards. A moment later, white-hot fire gouted from the turret and a string of secondary explosions began to detonate inside the hull, as the panzer's ammunition began to cook off.

"Stop gawking and keep loading, you big lummox!" Miller shouted.

Nelson snapped out of his momentary daze and grabbed another round, reloading the eighty-eight, and Miller gave the order to fire the instant the weapon was loaded. After yanking on the firing lever, Nelson reached over and took the last shell from the ammunition crate, then loaded the cannon again.

"That was the last round!" he hollered.

Miller gave the order and Nelson fired the cannon again, then peered around the gun shield and saw a second tank burning. The panzer had tried to manoeuvre around the first tank, and Miller had delivered a flanking shot, punching a glowing hole right through the middle of the second Panzer III's chassis.

"Open another crate!" Miller ordered. "Hurry, blast it!"

Nelson stumbled over smoking spent brass casings trying to find an ammunition crate marked *Panzergranaten*, but every time he illuminated one with the torch's beam, he was disappointed.

"I think we're out of AP!" he shouted.

"Grab anything! We'll be dead meat in seconds if that Panzer IV finds us!"

Nelson jabbed the end of his knife under the lid of a crate and pried it free. Clipping the lit torch to his webbing, he pulled out a shell and stepped around the debris, thrusting the fresh round into the breech. Miller worked the traversing wheel, shifting the cannon slightly.

"Need another flare!" Miller said. "Can't bloody see anything through all the smoke."

Nelson stepped around the gun and reloaded the flare pistol, firing another flare high into the air over the runway. The instant the flare popped, Nelson spotted the two remaining panzers - both of them were swinging wide around the runway, well out of the eighty-eight's line of fire, and bringing their turret guns to bear.

"Panzers, two o'clock!" he yelled.

Miller frantically spun the traversing wheel, and the gun slowly came about, but it was too late. Both tanks opened fire with their machine guns, and a fusillade of slugs ripped through the tent, glancing off the cannon's gun shield, tearing through the thin metal body of the German half-track, and smashing through the empty ammunition crates. Nelson shuddered to think what would happen if a tracer penetrated a live round in one of the full crates. He probably wouldn't even know what happened before the blast turned him to bloody hash.

There was a *crack* and sparks flew from the rear of the half-track, followed instantly by the report of a tank's main gun. Bits of red-hot metal ignited the back wall of the tent, which began to smoulder.

"Fire, you big oaf! Fire!" Miller hollered, and Nelson stepped away from the breech block and tripped the eighty-eight's firing lever. The shell smashed into the circling Panzer III, tearing through its engine compartment. Nelson saw several figures bail out of the tank as it caught fire.

"Load, load!" Miller cried out, traversing to bring the gun to bear on the large Panzer IV, moving at speed to come around their flank. The barrel of the eighty-eight hit the other side of the tent fabric and caught it, obscuring Miller's view.

"Christ, I can't bloody see!" Miller shouted.

There was a heavy report, and a shell cut through the tent and out the other side faster than the blink of an eye. A moment later, there was an explosion a hundred yards to their rear.

"The tent - cut the tent!" Miller demanded.

Nelson grabbed the next shell and all but threw it into the breech, before scrambling over the rear of the gun carriage and attacking the tent fabric with his knife, cutting it away with great hacking sweeps of the blade. Three hundred yards away, the Panzer IV opened fire with its co-axial machine gun, the tracers zipping all around Nelson, several glancing off the eighty-eight's gun barrel and the shield next to him. A ricochet plucked at his sleeve, another smacked into one of the magazine pouches at his hip.

At last, the tent cloth was sliced away, and Nelson stumbled around Miller and over the gun carriage, pulling the firing lever as soon as his fingers found it. The shot arced out and plowed up a great furrow of earth behind and well beyond the panzer, whose commander had shrewdly ordered the driver to increase speed as soon as he saw the eighty-eight had a clear line of sight.

Nelson turned and picked up another shell, but before he could load the gun, there was a terrible blast. The explosion picked him up and slammed him against the tailgate of the half-track. Ears ringing, he groaned and struggled to his hands and knees, squinting through the smoke and dust swirling through what remained of the tent. He saw Miller lying across the rear gun carriage, moving feebly, and there was a great rent torn in the gun shield. Nelson crawled to Miller, and saw the gunner's right leg was gone below the knee. Several other shrapnel wounds along his right side were slowly oozing blood.

Dazedly, Miller looked at Nelson. "Prop me next to the firing lever, then load and aim."

Nelson shook his head. "I can't work this bloody monster, that's why I brought you along!"

"You'll do fine," Miller mumbled through bloody lips. "Now, do as I say, or we're both goners."

Nelson stumbled to his feet and gently propped Miller up against the eighty-eight's pedestal, placing the wounded man's hand on the firing lever. Then Nelson turned, searching for the shell he'd had in his hands. He saw it lying several feet away, picked it up, and staggered to the gun's breech. He pushed the shell home, the breech nipping at his fingers as it closed automatically.

"It's loaded!" he shouted over the ringing in his ears. "Now what?"

"Traverse the gun!" Miller gasped. "Lead just a touch and be light with the wheel, it's more sensitive than you think."

Nelson peered through the eighty-eight's gunsight. The panzer continued to circle them, and he spun the traversing wheel to bring the weapon about. A stream of MG fire arced towards him, the bullets hammering at the gun shield, and the panzer's 75mm howitzer boomed once more. Nelson braced himself for the worst, but the shell flashed by, missing the gun shield by a hair's breadth.

He had only one chance. Nelson took a deep breath, forcing himself to focus, to think of the great cannon as nothing more than a gigantic rifle, the panzer as nothing but a target. He spun the traversing wheel, bringing the sight around, matching the speed of the encircling panzer and placing the aim-point right above the lead sprocket wheel.

"Now!" he shouted.

The eighty-eight roared, the cannon slamming back in recoil. Nelson stayed on the sights, knowing the next few seconds meant his life or death and there was no use not watching the show. The shell crossed the distance from gun to tank in a split second, and the shell struck a third of the way back along the top of the treads. There was a flash as the high-explosive shell detonated upon impact, and bits of twisted metal spun through the smoke and dust. When the tank was visible again, Nelson saw it had slewed around, the right-hand track completely mangled, flames licking from a rent in the hull. A lone figure struggled out of the turret hatch, his legs aflame. The German tumbled down off the side of the panzer's hull and into the sand, where he feebly rolled around, putting out the flames.

Nelson turned away from the gun sight. "Miller, you keen devil! We got them all!"

There was no reply from the gunner. Nelson pointed the electric torch at Miller's motionless form, and saw the man's eyes staring, unblinking, his hand still gripping the firing lever.

TWENTY-TWO

The Airfield
November 18th, 0230 Hours

The last of the gunfire had stopped by the time Nelson carried Miller's body back to where the tankers were congregated. A handful of German prisoners knelt in the sand, hands behind their heads, guarded by Herring and several other men with leveled rifles. Among the German prisoners was the *Luftwaffe* officer who'd been with Steiner when he'd first addressed the British prisoners. One of the British tankers was binding the German officer's leg with a battle dressing as blood seeped through from a bullet wound in the thigh.

Chalmers, standing nearby and talking with Herring, saw Nelson approach. By the light of the burning panzers, Nelson saw the officer's look of sorrow when he realized what Nelson carried.

"Oh, blast it all," Chalmers cursed. "The poor fellow."

"He brewed up three of 'em," Nelson said, as he lowered Miller's body to the ground at Chalmers' feet. "The big one got him with a shell, but he talked me through killing the last panzer. He even managed to fire the cannon before he died."

Chalmers knelt next to his gunner's body and laid a hand on Miller's chest for a moment. "When our tank was knocked out, he was willing to fight to the end with nothing more than a Bren. The panzer that killed him, it knocked us out and captured us this morning."

"The surviving Jerries are coming in," Herring called out.

Nelson turned. Several figures approached from the direction of the last two panzers, moving unsteadily with hands raised above their heads. Two of the men supported a third, who stumbled along with burned legs too weak to bear his weight.

Chalmers and Nelson stood, and along with the rest of the British, waited in silence, unmoving, until the four Germans all but collapsed at their feet. The men were blackened and scorched, their faces smeared with oil and soot. The man with the burned legs, a junior officer by his insignia, looked up at Chalmers with an agonized expression.

"*Kameraden*," the German whispered. "*Nicht schiessen!*"

Chalmers stared at the German, his eyes narrowed, jaw clenched. He slowly pointed at Miller's body.

"My *Kameraden*," Chalmers whispered. He pointed towards the eighty-eight at the other end of the airfield, then at Nelson, and back to Miller. "*Schiessen.*"

The German officer swallowed, then shook his head. "*Nicht schiessen, bitte. Es ist Krieg.*"

Nelson unslung his MP-40 and held it out to Chalmers. "Up to you, sir. He was your mate."

Chalmers reached out for the weapon, but as he touched it, he drew his hand away and shook his head.

"No, Corporal, I won't do that. It was a clean fight. The poor chap is right, it's just war. At least, I think that's what the blighter said."

The burned German let out a gasp of relief and nodded thanks. One of the other British tankers approached, holding a German medical kit.

"Shall I attend to his burns, sir?" the tanker asked.

Chalmers nodded. "Yes, do what you can for him, thanks."

Just then, there were a couple of shouts from off to the east, and everyone turned, weapons brought up to bear. Nelson heard voices with familiar accents calling out, asking permission to approach the airfield.

"Sounds like the Kiwis from Desert Group!" he exclaimed.

Out of the darkness, six men emerged. Nelson recognized two of them as Captain Clarke and one of his New Zealanders. The other four were Sergeant Peabody and three of the Commandos from his squad.

Chalmers stepped forward and saluted Clarke. "Lieutenant Chalmers, sir. Ranking officer here. We're all that's left of Major Meade's squadron."

Clarke returned Chalmers' salute, then noticed Nelson and Herring. "You lads, did your captain or lieutenant survive the action?"

Nelson nodded. "They scarpered to the west after being attacked by some Jerry armoured cars. Me and Herring here, and our Kiwi - beg pardon sir - we drew fire to give the others time to leg it. Lost the truck and your man, and we wound up in the bag, at least until we cut ourselves loose and broke out this lot."

Clark nodded, his expression indicating how impressed he was at their actions. "Our flanking element ran smack into the panzers in that hidden ravine. Captain Moody was killed almost immediately, his other armoured cars and the two lead trucks destroyed as well. But the ravine was so narrow, once the other vehicles were destroyed, the smoke and debris meant we could back out and retreat. We laid up a few miles away, but when we heard all the shooting, we decided to take the chance and come in, thinking Meade's lads had merely fallen back and come in under cover of darkness. But now, it looks like that wasn't the case."

Over the next several minutes, Nelson and Chalmers filled Clarke in on what had happened over the course of the day, as well as the escape and ensuing battle that night. When their debrief was complete, Clarke looked equal parts horrified at the British losses from the initial attack, and amazed at the audacity with which Nelson and Herring had executed their plan.

"Well lads," Clarke said after a moment's reflection, "all that's left is finding Eldred, Price, and the other survivors, and hoping Steiner doesn't get to them first."

"He's got a Panzer IV and three armoured cars," Chalmers cautioned. "We've got no armour to counter them."

"What about that eighty-eight?" Sergeant Peabody asked. "That'd get the job done right bloody quick."

Nelson shook his head. "The half-track didn't look like it had moved in months, and even if it worked, it'd be too bloody slow. That gun is a right monster."

"What if we tried to tow it with the remaining Jerry lorries?" Chalmers asked.

Nelson frowned. "Which lorries?"

"Of course," Chalmers said. "You were laid out when they brought you back. Those light anti-tank guns, the ones you lot were taking on to the west out there, they were towed by Jerry lorries. You were carried here in one when they brought the AT guns back in. We saw Steiner take off with one of them, but there are others parked over by the panzer leaguer."

A few minutes later, Chalmers, Clarke, Peabody, and Nelson were examining the Krupp-Protze transports. Still hooked up to each was a Pak 36 anti-tank gun. A fourth gun, blackened and damaged, sat to the side. Nelson shook his head.

"The half-track back there is a right monster, and you need something that big to tow that great bloody cannon. These trucks look a bit weedy for that kind of job." He turned and looked to Chalmers. "These guns, how good are they?"

"Good enough to brew up a Crusader at combat ranges," he replied. "They aren't much different than the two-pounders on our tanks. Get them close, especially with a flank or rear shot, and they'll do a proper job on that Panzer IV."

"The question is," Peabody said, "can we get close enough? If we're approaching in nothing but lorries and recce trucks, a bloody MG can rip us apart."

Clarke smiled. "Why would they shoot at their own vehicles? I think with a little prestidigitation, we can get in close before we're rumbled."

"But how do we know where Eldred and the others are?" Chalmers asked.

Nelson remembered the wounded *Luftwaffe* officer among the German prisoners. He smiled.

"No worries about that one," Nelson replied. "Leave it to me."

TWENTY-THREE

The Ravine
November 18th, 0600 Hours

The first howitzer shell arced in and detonated twenty yards to Lynch's right. A few bits of shrapnel hissed overhead, while sand and pulverized rock fragments fell around him like rain. He squinted into the early-morning sun and spotted the Panzer IV a thousand yards away. The muzzle lit up with flame and smoke again, and another shell arced in, this one detonating well behind and to the left.

Lynch turned to Lance Corporal White, who was serving as his loader. "Not much we can do about that beast from here now, is there?"

White nodded and peered through a pair of field glasses. "The armoured cars are swinging to the south. I think they're going to try and flank us. Hold on, they're-"

The impacts of 20mm cannon shells all around them were followed a moment later by the sound of the autocannons' reports. After a few seconds, the barrage subsided, only to be replaced by the patter of dozens of bullets smacking into the sand and rock. A 7.92mm slug *thwacked* into a stone a yard from Lynch's left elbow, and a mashed fragment of copper and lead bounced onto the back of his hand, still warm enough to make him shake it away like it was a biting insect.

Another howitzer shell impacted to Lynch's left, this one on the other side of the narrow ravine. Lynch looked over there and saw Bowen and Johnson, partially obscured by the debris still hanging in the air, trying to burrow themselves even deeper into their shallow two-man foxhole. Lynch's own fighting position was barely a foot deep and just long enough for him to fit inside while prone, and White's wasn't much better. The sand around them was soft enough, but it was only a few inches deep. Underneath, there was a lot of dense gravel and hard stone that had to be dug through, usually with the use of a pick to pry the mixture loose before shoveling it away.

As a combination of howitzer shells, autocannon rounds, and machine gun bullets continued to rain down around them, White looked to Lynch. "This is just to pin us down. They've got to be moving infantry against us."

Lynch nodded. "Aye, to be sure. But where might they be now?"

Just then, a single bullet smacked into the ground in front of them, and both men - combat veterans more than familiar with the behavior of ricochets - realized the shot came from their far right.

"Well, there we go," White muttered.

The two men shifted in their fighting positions. Lynch left the Boys anti-tank rifle where it sat facing the east, and picked up his trusty Thompson. White readied his own Thompson, and the two of them searched the terrain to their south. Soon enough, a German exposed himself just long enough to fire a rifle, the bullet cracking between the two Commandos. Lynch aimed and fired a short burst from his Thompson, but the figure was gone before the first bullets landed.

"This is sure to be bad," Lynch said.

"If we break, there's no cover, and we'll be taking fire from that damn panzer and those cars the whole time," White replied.

To the south, there was more movement, and the first burst from an MG-34 chopped up the sand in front of their fighting positions.

"They're going to fire and manoeuvre until they're right on top of us!" White shouted over the sound of another howitzer shell exploding nearby.

The crack of a Lee-Enfield to the north was immediately followed by a figure to the south flinging up their arms from the impact of a bullet. Both men turned and looked behind them. A slight puff of dust was rising from Bowen's position, and a second shot passed over their heads.

"If we're going to move, we've got to move now," Lynch said.

White nodded. Lynch flashed hand signals to Bowen and Johnson, who made a gesture in acknowledgment. A third bullet cracked past overhead, and there was a shout of alarm from the south. Lynch and White jumped up, each man grabbing one end of the Boys rifle, and they took off to the west, running almost parallel to the ravine. Rifle and machine gun bullets snapped all around them, and another shell exploded near the fighting positions they'd just abandoned, but the two men covered fifty yards before skidding behind a small outcropping of rock near the ravine's edge.

White leaned out from behind their cover and cut loose with a full magazine from his Thompson, driving back the German infantry who'd tried to use the Commandos' retreat as an opportunity to advance. Bullets forced him to duck back and as he reloaded, panting from their run and the effort of carrying the Boys rifle, he nodded towards the west.

"Get that bloody great rifle ready. I saw those cars swinging around. They're going to try and cut off our retreat."

Lynch cursed. The four men along the ridgeline had agreed to stay back and delay any German advance while the other three trucks pushed west through the ravine. One truck remained, almost directly below where they now were, but if they let the armoured cars get past, the Germans would have both ends of the ravine bottled up.

Seating the Boys rifle properly on its bipod, Lynch went prone and squirmed to the right, edging the muzzle of the rifle around the outcropping.

"Keep those bloody Jerries off me arse now," he muttered.

Behind him, White fired off a few short bursts. "Easier said than done. They're like jerobas, hopping up and down behind every blasted rock."

A moment later, one of the smaller, four-wheeled armoured cars came into view. Although the range was about three hundred yards, Lynch took the shot anyway, as the car was moving slowly and it was a flank shot. He didn't see whether his shot had any effect or not, so Lynch fired twice more, each shot hammering his shoulder more painfully than the last. He hadn't had time to stuff a pair of woolen socks into his battledress as padding against the recoil, and the Boys rifle kicked like an angry mule.

Two more shots emptied the Boys' five-round magazine, and Lynch ripped it away, swearing as he moved his right arm, shoulder throbbing. But the armoured car was now stationary, a thin curl of smoke rising from its engine compartment. Further on, the other two cars swiveled their turrets and returned fire, driving Lynch back behind cover as cannon shells punched massive trenches in the sand and struck the rock outcropping with punishing force.

"They're bloody well mad at you now, mate!" White laughed as he reloaded again. Lynch saw a small pile of spent magazines near the man's feet.

"Jerries still pressing us?" Lynch asked.

"If it wasn't for this Thompson and Rhys over there trying to ventilate their uniforms, you'd have a Boche bayonet up yer bum right now," White replied.

"We better get to the truck, because if we don't get out of here, that bloody great steel monster's going to climb up the rise, or make its way into the ravine, and then one way or another, we're done for," Lynch said.

Across the ravine, Lynch saw Bowen duck down to reload, while Johnson fired a long burst from a plundered MP-40, raking fire back and forth towards the Germans to the south. As Lynch watched, a shell burst a few feet from Johnson, and when the debris settled, the redheaded spotter was sprawled half out of the foxhole, the machine pistol lying several feet from his hands.

"Bastards! Johnson's been hit!" Lynch cried.

White turned from firing, and they both saw Bowen pulling Johnson down into cover. A second shell landed a few yards from the first, kicking a plume of shattered rock and sand into the air.

"This isn't good!" White shouted over the noise.

"Bowen's not going to be able to get Johnson down the ravine wall if he's wounded," Lynch replied, choosing not to think the spotter might have been killed.

Chancing a peek around the outcropping, Lynch saw the two operational armoured cars continuing on towards the end of the ravine, now well out of effective range of the Boys rifle, but also well beyond bothering to deal with two enemy infantrymen to their rear. In looking to the east, he no longer saw the panzer; it was below his line of sight, close to the bottom of the rise. Towards the horizon, however, Lynch detected plumes of dust coming towards them.

"The cars have moved on, so it's now or never. Looks like Jerry reinforcements arriving. We need to move," Lynch told White.

"What about Rhys?" White asked.

Lynch waved to get the sniper's attention as the Welshman fired another round towards the German infantry. Bowen looked his way, and Lynch indicated Bowen needed to make a break for it, and that they'd lay down cover fire. At first Bowen refused, but when Lynch pointed at the German reinforcements approaching, he saw Bowen nod.

"Alright, make sure you're full now," Lynch said.

White nodded and switched magazines. "This is my last one."

Lynch dug two from his ammunition pouch. "Here, I'm still flush."

The two men shifted out from behind cover and opened fire on the Germans. Working their triggers carefully, each man nursed short bursts from their weapons, putting down aimed fire anywhere they saw movement. Out of the corner of his eye, Lynch saw Bowen, his rifle slung, staggering away from the foxhole, his spotter draped across his shoulder.

"Bloody hell!" Lynch exclaimed. "The wee bugger'll snap his ankles doing that!"

Bullets kicked puffs of dust all around him, but Bowen made it to the edge of the ravine, where a rope anchored into the rock hung down to the bottom. Under fire, Bowen pulled the line up, tied it around Johnson's waist, and then eased the wounded man over the edge. The face of the ravine wasn't vertical, just very steep, and handling the rope carefully, Bowen eased his spotter down a few yards at a time.

The Germans apparently saw this, and strangely, the firing towards Bowen slacked off. Reloading, Lynch leaned back out from behind cover with his Thompson at the ready, but he saw no targets.

"Huns must be so impressed, they didn't have the heart to shoot him!" White declared.

"I think they saw their friends arriving, and didn't think it was worth the bother to stick their heads up. Let's make the most of it!" Lynch replied.

The two men moved to the edge of the ravine and grabbed onto their own ropes. Lynch eyed the Boys rifle and cursed. There was no way he was carrying it down now, so he fired a round from his Thompson into the Boys rifle's receiver, denting the mechanism and rendering the weapon useless. Looking across, Lynch saw Bowen had started making his way down the ravine using his own line, and he turned to White with a grin.

"Alright," Lynch said, "race you to the bottom!"

From the east came the sharp report of a high-velocity cannon.

And then another.

And another.

TWENTY-FOUR

The Ravine
November 18th, 0615 Hours

Steiner peered into the gloom of the ravine as his eight-wheeled armoured car followed its smaller cousin into the shadows. High above, a slash of early-morning sky provided little illumination, and there was no sign of the sunrise ahead to the east, with all the twists and turns between them and the ravine's end. Ahead of the light armoured car, the three crewmen of the disabled car scouted ahead on foot, each man carrying an MP-40 at the ready, one man lighting the way with an electric torch.

Five minutes ago he'd gotten a transmission from Mueller. Just as the *Feldwebel* was about to take his panzer into the ravine, he'd radioed Steiner to report seeing vehicles approaching from the east. Not armour, but what appeared to be transport trucks. Steiner thought it was strange, but then it occurred to him that Hasek might have sent the transports in anticipation of more prisoners, and perhaps to pass along any information he might have gleaned from the prisoners they'd already captured.

He'd lost contact with Mueller moments ago, no doubt because down within the confines of the ravine, radio transmissions were all but impossible. Steiner knew Mueller would move forward into the ravine slowly and shell anything suspicious, driving the Commandos west and right into Steiner and his armoured cars. The 20mm autocannons and coaxial machine guns of both cars were loaded and ready. Steiner even had a machine pistol, passed up from inside the car, sitting on the edge of his hatch in case he needed it.

One of the men scouting twenty metres ahead of the first scout car shouted an alarm and fired a long burst into the ravine. The report, magnified and reflected from the stone all around them, rolled around like thunder for a moment before dying away. A moment later, the deep-throated reply of a light machine gun rattled back at them, and several slugs bounced off the hull of Steiner's armoured car, ricocheting in from an unseen assailant. Steiner ducked down, but kept his head above the lip of the hatch. The ravine was no place to limit one's field of view to a few small vision blocks.

Steiner turned to Werner. "Load AP into the cannon, and fire a few bursts from the MG. See if we can't send a few ricochets their way."

As Werner carried out his orders, Steiner keyed his radio. "Car Two, can you see anything?"

"Nothing so far. The scouts say they spotted a couple of Tommies on foot."

"Push forward then. Load your cannon with armour-piercing. It'll stay intact if it ricochets around corners."

The two armoured cars moved forward at a slow walking pace, taking the twists and turns in the ravine as widely as possible to give the gunners the best angles. The scouts caught glimpses of the British several more times and exchanged fire with them, but as best as Steiner could tell, they caused no casualties. More than once, the only reply from the British was a hand grenade tossed around an outcropping of rock, and by the time the debris settled and the scouts peeked out from around whatever cover had been nearby, the British had retreated.

"I don't like this," Werner muttered, eyes glued to his weapon sight.

Steiner said nothing, but he knew something was amiss. Were they trying to find a good place to make a last stand? Steiner hoped not, because not only would it be a senseless act, he'd no doubt lose more men before it was over. Furthermore, the British had to know by now the panzer was moving in from the east, squeezing them from the other side of the ravine.

Hoping for a report, Steiner tried to get Mueller on the radio again, but there was no response. He realized he hadn't heard the distant *krump* of an exploding howitzer shell for several minutes now. There was no way the panzer would have run out of high explosive shells so quickly; Mueller was an experienced commander, and wouldn't make that mistake. He hoped instead the *Feldwebel* was in contact with their reinforcements, perhaps trying to get them organized in support of the battle plan.

Glancing behind him, Steiner didn't see any daylight. He had lost track of how far into the ravine they'd progressed. Five hundred metres? A kilometre? It couldn't have been two. The rock walls of the ravine climbed up almost vertically around him, the monotonous stone playing tricks with his senses. Steiner found it oddly claustrophobic, and wondered what it would take to knock one of the ravine walls in and bury them all. What if the British had concealed a demolition charge, and were waiting for the two cars to get within range? Would he rather die in an explosion that shattered his vehicle and dismembered his body, or would he prefer a rockslide that crushed the car like a tin can under tons of falling rock, reducing him to a grotesque paste? Steiner had once seen the body of a French infantryman that'd been run over by a column of panzers during the drive for Calais. Smashed into the rut caused by the panzers' treads, the corpse had been almost comical, a deflated caricature of a human being, like something out of an American cartoon.

A rapid series of explosions right around the next bend fifty metres ahead snapped Steiner out of his daydreaming. A cloud of dust and pulverized rock drifted out from around the bend, and a lone figure, limping and bloody, stumbled into view. It was one of his Brandenburgers, and the man dropped to his knees before falling on his face, limp in death.

Steiner keyed his radio mic. "Car Two, advance and engage!"

The driver of the SdKfz 222 gunned the engine, and the four-wheeled armoured car pulled ahead, the car's gunner firing several short bursts into the cloud of dust still hanging in the air, obscuring the turn. A sudden thought turned Steiner's blood cold.

"Wait!" he shouted into the mic. "Don't take the turn!"

There was the whipcrack sound of a high-velocity cannon firing, and the unmistakable *clang* of an armour-piercing round punching through steel plate. Steiner saw a large chunk of the lead car's right-front tyre leap into the air, torn from the wheel. Frantic, Steiner saw the car's gunner firing the machine gun like mad, and it took Steiner only a second to realize the problem: the anti-tank gun was firing at point-blank range in front of the car, and the turret-mounted weapons couldn't depress far enough to engage.

Even as Steiner reached for his machine pistol, a part of his mind couldn't help admiring the Commandos' cunning.

They'd wiped out the scouts and obscured the bend in the ravine just long enough to bring up a gun, and they'd positioned it so close that at the moment they had a shot, they were safe from return fire. An audacious move, one that certainly put Steiner and his men on their back heel.

The driver of the lead car attempted to back away from the bend and gain some distance, but the wrecked tyre caused the car to lurch and wobble, making progress slow. The sound of a second shot from the gun reverberated off the ravine walls, and the machine-gun fire from the 222 immediately stopped. There was a third report, and then a fourth, and the car stopped moving and began to burn. Steiner stood immobile in his turret hatch, staring at the destroyed car only fifty metres ahead of him. He watched as an arm, sheathed in flames, frantically tried lifting the anti-grenade screen covering the car's open turret, but to no avail. After a few horrifying seconds, the arm dropped, still in flames, and hung over the rear of the turret.

Steiner swallowed. "Back us out of here, now!" he said, his voice hoarse. "Werner, lay down covering fire. Use the autocannon."

The car's rear-facing driver began to move the car back, and Werner began firing short bursts of four or five rounds at a time, the solid, armour-piercing shells smacking against the rocks and careening around the bend. Steiner rewarded himself with a brief sigh of relief. There was no way the British would risk coming after them with that gun, even if they could get it past the burning wreck taking up most of the room at the head of that bend.

A fist-sized rock glanced off the top of the turret right in front of Steiner. Thinking his wild fears of being buried alive were about to come to pass, he looked up in alarm, half-expecting to see a mass of boulders rushing down the ravine wall.

Instead, he saw a dozen British soldiers in a mix of uniforms, all pointing weapons at him. One of them, the large, thuggish-looking Commando he'd interrogated the day before, stood right at the edge, wearing a menacing grin while holding a machine pistol in one hand and a grenade in the other. As Steiner watched, the Commando pulled the grenade's pin with his teeth and spat it into the ravine, then held the grenade as if ready to lob it right into Steiner's open hatch. Several of the other men around him also held grenades at the ready.

""Ello, Fritz." the Commando said. "Fancy a game of catch?"

Steiner ordered the driver to halt the car, and then kept his hands well away from both the machine pistol and the handle of the turret hatch.

The Commando nodded to someone out of sight. Almost immediately, a pair of arms thrust Huber to the edge of the ravine, their grip on his webbing the only thing keeping the *Feldwebel* from tumbling to his death.

"I am sorry, *Hauptmann*," Huber said. "They attacked with trucks mounting machine guns. They were on top of us before we could react."

"How many men are alive?" Steiner asked.

"Myself and three others," Huber replied.

"And Mueller?"

Huber shook his head. "They used our own Pak 36s. Mueller died when his tank burned."

Steiner closed his eyes for a moment. Four men left in Huber's squad, plus the three other men in the armoured car. *I can save eight of us, at least,* he thought.

There was a tug on his pants leg, and Steiner glanced down at Werner. The gunner had a machine pistol in his hands.

"Give us the order, *Hauptmann*." Werner said, his voice steady.

Steiner looked back up. From around the front of the burning car up ahead, a trio of Commandos wheeled forward their anti-tank gun, setting it up so its muzzle was pointed right as his turret. Steiner immediately recognized it as a captured *Panzerbüchse* 41 squeeze bore, probably one of the very guns he'd brought with him to the *Bersaglieri* outpost several months ago. Steiner found himself chuckling softly at the notion of being defeated by his own weapons.

"*Hauptmann*, are you okay?" Werner asked.

Steiner gave his *Gefreiter* a smile. "Put down the gun, Werner. We're done fighting, at least for now."

Standing up straight in the turret hatch, Steiner raised his hands and looked up at the men who'd beaten him.

"Alright, chaps. You've got me."

The Commando with the grenade smiled broadly, then glanced at the armed bomb in his hand.

"Oi, lads! Any of you lot 'ave a grenade pin? I threw mine away."

TWENTY-FIVE

Mersa Matruh Airfield, Egypt
December 1st, 1930 Hours

Lynch stepped out of the hangar serving as their barracks for the last twenty-four hours and made his way to the plane waiting on the runway. The hangar was the same one used by their unit over a month ago, when they'd arrived in North Africa under cover of darkness. Now, they were departing under the same conditions, about to embark on a two-day journey back to Scotland.

Behind him, others of his squad emerged single file. Their original twelve-man squad was now reduced to nine. Johnson had survived his wounds, but they were serious enough to warrant shipping him out the day they'd arrived back in Mersa Matruh over a week ago. Stillwell, who'd been shot in the leg during the assault on the *Bersaglieri* outpost, had been shipped out almost three weeks ago. Brooks, killed instantly by a round from an anti-tank gun, had been buried out in the desert.

Still, Lynch counted his squad lucky. Sergeant Peabody's squad had lost eight men killed or wounded in the last few days, and Donovan's squad had suffered so many casualties from the operation in October that those few who remained had taken the place of casualties in Peabody's squad, with the wounded men from both squads sent back to Mersa Matruh and eventually off to Blighty along with Stillwell.

Handing his Thompson to McTeague, already aboard the plane, Lynch climbed in and settled into a seat next to Nelson. The Englishman had become insufferably cocky since the events of the eighteenth, particularly with regards to having brewed up not one, but two of the large Panzer IVs.

Nelson turned to Lynch. "Well, if it ain't ol' pissy britches!"

Lynch punched Nelson in the shoulder. "I didn't piss me britches, you spotty arse."

"So says you! I bet a pint of the best porter you had a weak trickle running down your leg when we landed," Nelson shot back.

"I'll give you a trickle, old son!" Lynch snapped his fist down into Nelson's groin, eliciting a howl of pain and a flurry of blows on Lynch's shoulder, arm, and thigh.

"If you two keep acting like a couple of prats every time we climb into a bloody airplane," McTeague growled from the other end of the passenger compartment, "I'll start pushin' ye out without parachutes!"

"These lads causing trouble as usual, Sergeant?" Price asked as he climbed aboard.

"Nothin' I can't knock out of 'em, sir," McTeague replied.

Price found a seat, propping his Beretta machine pistol between his knees. "Well lads, I have news that may be of interest to you. Some of it's good, some bad."

"Let's have the good news first, sir," Lynch said.

"The rumors are true," Price replied. "We've managed to break the siege at Tobruk, and although the battle is far from over, it sounds like we're trading equal blows with Rommel's lads. HQ is confident that, given time, Crusader will be a success."

"Sounds brilliant to me," Lynch said. "What's the bad news?"

Price gave them a broad smile. "After all this hot sun and gritty sand, you'll be happy to know the weather back home is much cooler than when we left in October. In fact, it's downright brisk. The weather report I received today said it's snowing rather heavily back home."

McTeague let out a diabolical chuckle. "Sounds like the perfect weather for a good long march, Lieutenant. Just what the lads need to be proper soldiers again."

The plane's engines roared as the pilot prepared for takeoff, drowning out the curses and groans coming from inside the passenger compartment.

TWENTY-SIX

Mersa Matruh Airfield
December 2ⁿᵈ, 2300 Hours

Karl Steiner finished buttoning up the British battledress, and tightened the chin strap of his newly-acquired helmet. Satisfied it was secure, he looked down at his uniform and made sure no bloodstains were visible. To his left, Werner dragged the last of the sentries' bodies out of sight, covering them up with a nearby tarpaulin.

Steiner opened the bolt of the Lee-Enfield rifle in his hands, making sure there was a round in the chamber. Behind him stood Fromm, his last Brandenburger, who was also dressed in the uniform of a dead British soldier. Fromm tied a simple, loose knot around Huber's hands, and made sure the other three men of the *Feldwebel*'s squad, along with his armoured car's driver, were similarly bound. When their preparations were completed, Fromm gave Steiner a nod.

"Alright, easy now," Steiner whispered in English. "We're just three lads from ol' Blighty, escorting a few Jerries from one end of the airfield to the other."

The eight men began to walk, Steiner leading them with his rifle held ready, the two remaining Brandenburgers in

British uniform bringing up the rear. As the minutes passed, they crossed paths with several genuine British soldiers and airmen, but an easy word or quip from Steiner had them on their way without trouble.

An hour later, they were cutting through the airfield's perimeter fence. Steiner took one last look back at the airfield before slipping between the wires and pulling them straight behind him. A few miles away, he knew of a cache left by the Brandenburgers who'd been working with the Egyptian spies. Forged papers, currency, more weapons, and even explosives had been hidden away by his fallen brothers.

Time to go to work, Steiner thought to himself, and slipped away into the night.

Author's Note

The inspiration for this book came from two historical missions carried out in November 1941 in support of Operation Crusader. The first, Operation Flipper, was a raid by No. 11 Commando designed to disrupt Axis command and control on the eve of Crusader, primarily through attacking Rommel's headquarters and either capturing or killing him. Flipper was a disaster from the very beginning, and the mission's poor luck only grew worse, finally ending with almost every man who'd made it ashore being captured or killed. The second mission was the first formal operation carried out by the Special Air Service, involving an airborne insertion during extremely bad weather resulting in the majority of the SAS men also being captured or killed.

Although the daring and fighting spirit of the men carrying out these raids is without question, the missions made evident the fact that Commando-style missions were extremely high-risk affairs, and the slightest bit of bad luck could (and often did) result in disasters. The degree of risk involved was only heightened by the lack of understanding as to which missions were well-suited to forces like the Commandos, the LRDG, and the SAS. Furthermore, these forces were still in their infancy, the men still largely untested, their training and techniques not yet perfected. And, as a result, brave men died or spent a large portion of the war as POWs.

On the other hand, the tank battles in this book were inspired primarily by two books. The first is Major Robert Crisp's BRAZEN CHARIOTS, a memoir of Crisp's involvement in Operation Crusader. Crisp was a troop commander in the 4th Royal Tank Regiment, commanding a lend-lease M3 "Honey" Stuart light tank against Panzer IIIs and IVs. The second book is Lt. Col. Cyril Joly's TAKE THESE MEN, a historical novel set over the course of the entire Desert Campaign, from battling the Italians to the surrender of the 15th Panzer Division. Joly was also an officer in the British Eighth Army, and he and Crisp served together during the war. As of this writing, only Crisp's memoir is currently in print, although Joly's novel is available through used book dealers. Both are incredibly visceral, engaging stories of the epic, far-ranging battles back and forth across the expanse of North Africa. Many of the little details – such as the radio protocols of British tank units – came from these two works, and any errors in fact are entirely my own.

As always, I want to thank everyone who has read the previous entries in the COMMANDO series, and I hope you also enjoyed this latest adventure. If you have the time and inclination, please take a moment to leave a review (or reviews) of these stories on Amazon or wherever you prefer. Books sell on the strength of their product reviews, and the feedback I receive from reviews helps me write the sorts of stories my readers most enjoy.

And finally, on an entirely personal note, I want to dedicate this book to the memory of Bailey, my feline writing companion. Bailey would sit with me for hours upon hours while I typed away, purring contentedly on a nearby chair or even curled up around the corner of my laptop. As any writer can tell you, this can be a lonely business, and an animal companion can be a great comfort during frustrating bouts of writer's block or while trying to meet a looming deadline. Bailey had been with me since before the beginning of my first novel, and it breaks my heart to know I'll be starting the next without him by my side. So long, little buddy – it won't be the same without you.

Contact Me

My Blog: postmodernpulp.com

Facebook: facebook.com/jack.badelaire

Twitter: @jbadelaire

Email: j.e.badelaire@gmail.com

Mailing list for new book announcements:

http://postmodernpulps.blogspot.com/p/mailing-list.html

Works by Jack Badelaire:

The COMMANDO Series (WW2 Adventure Pulp)

>   *Operation Arrowhead*

>   *Operation Bedlam*

>   *Operation Cannibal*

>   *Operation Dervish*

>   *The Train to Calais* (short story)

The HANGMAN Series ('70s Men's Adventure)

>   *San Francisco Slaughter*

Killer Instincts (vigilante revenge thriller)

Renegade's Revenge (western novella)

Spiders and Flies (fantasy novella)

Nanok and the Tower of Sorrows (fantasy short story)

Rivalry – A Ghost Story (horror short story)

Hatchet Force Journal #1 *(fanzine)*

8717249R00134

Printed in Great Britain
by Amazon.co.uk, Ltd.,
Marston Gate.